MW01128349

THE FIFTY-TWO WEEK CHRONICLES

JOSLYN WESTBROOK

Fifth Avenue Publications

To my family - you are my greatest strength and my reason WHY...

Part One

"Maybe You Have To Let Go Of Who You Are To Become Who You Will Be."

Carrie Bradshaw - *Sex and the City*

CHAPTER 1

I fucking *hate* Mondays. And yes, I do realize most people on planet Earth also hate Mondays, but not as much as I do. No, most hate this day of the week because it means their bombastic weekend is over, or it signifies the inevitable commencement of an appalling work week, or some hate it because they party too damn much each weekend and subsequently battle a brutal Monday hangover. But as for me, my hatred for Monday far exceeds any one of those prissy explanations. Everything bad that's ever happened to me has happened on a Monday. And I mean *everything*.

Case in point: a chronological list of every bad event in my life that has occurred on a Monday:

1. Susie Q, my pet hamster, choked on a marble and died.

2. While roller skating, I fell, after tripping on a bump in the sidewalk, and broke my ankle.

3. My period started—at school. I was wearing a white mini skirt.

4. Michael Zane, the hottest guy in school, dumped me in front of everyone inside the lunchroom cafeteria.

5. During a talent show competition, I slipped on stage and chipped a tooth.

6. After much consideration, I ditched school for the first time—and got caught.

7. Received my first speeding ticket (but the cute officer asked me out on a date which nullified the experience).

8. I failed my first writing course in college—and my major was Journalism.

9. My heart was shattered by a cheating boyfriend.

10. I got fired.

To make matters worse, #9 and #10 just so happened to occur on the same Monday—which, by the way, is *today*. What are the fucking odds of that happening?

Perhaps the odds increased because the heartbreaking cheating-ass boyfriend is also my boss. Correction: he *was* my boss. You see Mr. Jerkboy thought it was his civil duty to fire me after I caught him screwing the crap out of his big-breasted, toothpick-waisted, grossly dimwitted, editorial assistant.

In *my* office!

How the hell could he do this to me? To *us*?

We met two years ago. It was my last year in college. Back then, I had applied to countless newspapers for an internship. All of them turned me down, probably because of my low GPA. But please don't judge me; NYU was a considerably arduous university. I majored in Journalism with a minor in Food Studies. Growing up, my mom and dad were sergeants in the U.S. Air Force. We traveled all over and I was the world-class epitome of a military brat. Our travels led to my obsession with food—not a manic type of an obsession. I mean the type of an obsession that makes a person appreciate the art of fine cuisine. And not only did I love eating food, I also loved writing about it. When most girls were writing "dear diary" entries about boy crushes, bitchy classmates, or evil parents, I was writing diary entries about how exceptional or how horrific a meal was.

Naturally, when I got accepted into NYU, I chose a major that would lead me to a career in writing—Journalism, and a minor that would suggest I am well-versed in the subject matter of food—Food Studies. I dreamed of one day becoming a food critic, but not any food critic. I dreamed of becoming a notably acclaimed food critic, known only by name. Michelin Star chefs would eagerly read reviews written by me—Penelope Monroe—in hopes they'd still be able to keep their well-merited star rating.

Many newspapers weren't ready to take on a new writer, let alone a new writer with a passion for food. However, as luck would have it, during a random online search one Saturday night, I came across the following:

THE HUDSON NEWS BEE *is looking for a college intern or recent college graduate who will work with our lead food critic and other food writers to craft our restaurant and food coverage for both online and print platforms. Candidates should be knowledgeable and passionate about food, write and report well, and be very organized. This is a full-time staff position with benefits. Applicants should email a resume, cover letter, and samples of their own food writing to*
foodeditor@hudsonmediagroup.com.

IT WAS as if me and that job opening had been majestically betrothed. Without hesitation, I made all of the required submissions: resume, cover letter, and a sample of food writing straight out of my own diary. I waited on pins and needles for some type of a reply.

And then it came.

Exactly four days later.

I had just returned from an early morning kick-me-hard-in-the-ass yoga class in Central Park. I was lounging comfortably on the hardwood living-room floor of the Harlem loft apartment my BFF Sebastian and I moved into earlier that spring. It was the first July in three years in which I was not enrolled in any NYU classes. My only assignment over the summer was to score an internship with a news-paper or a magazine. I had just about given up on *The Hudson News Bee* but just so happened to scroll through a barrage of emails on my iPad when I saw it.

An email from the editor.

FROM: HNB Food Editor
To: Penelope Monroe
Subject: Your Submission
Dear Penelope Monroe,

*Thank you for your recent submission for the open position. I am highly impressed with your writing as you demonstrate a high regard and passion for food. I would like to set up an in-person interview with you, Friday, 9am. Please bring with you **two** printed copies of a written review of a restaurant in SoHo called Cristofano Woods. It's extremely difficult to get a table there, but if you can pull this off, you'll walk into Friday's interview ahead of other candidates. Consider this your first assignment. Good Luck.*

I NEARLY PISSED my yoga pants *twice* after reading that email.

1) Interview in two days? Yay!

2) *Cristofano Woods*? Holy shit!

I mean, I had heard of *Cristofano Woods*. Who hadn't? It was a trendy new restaurant in SoHo that everyone had been talking about. Sebastian and I had talked about dining there for months, but couldn't make time in between my classes and his demanding job as a Public Relations Coordinator for Manifique, a thriving PR Firm. Plus, just as the editor mentioned in the email, getting a table at *Cristofano Woods* was near to impossible. I began to slightly freak out and remember thinking: how the hell can I pull this off?

Instinctively, I dialed Sebastian's cell phone. He always seemed to have answers when I was in distress. The two of us had been best friends since our first year at NYU. I remember our phone conversation as if it occurred just yesterday.

"Hello sexy," Sebastian said when he answered my call. "What's up?"

"You'll never guess what I'm calling about." I was sure the unconcealed excitement in my voice gave it away.

"Um...spare me the guessing games, sweetie. I've got a meeting in ten minutes, and I'd like to make a quick run to the little boys' room. I've gotta check out my threads. Demetrio Marks, the super-delicious model, is sure to make an appearance. You know firsthand how much I've been crushing on his gorgeousness," he said.

You see, when the two of us met during our first year at NYU, Sebastian had just come out to all of his friends and family. However, when I first met him I knew straight away he was gay and was totally fine with it. Every woman needs a gay best friend. It's like an unwritten rite of passage.

"Alrighty then," I said, "I promise not to hold you up. So," I took in a calming deep breath, "I totally scored an interview this Friday with *The Hudson News Bee!*" I screamed and did a happy dance all over the living-room floor.

"Shut the fuck up! That's so freaking awesome!" he said then paused for a few seconds. "Wait. Why do I feel like a scathing-ass caveat is about to be totally tossed my way right now?"

"You're so psychic." I laughed. "The scathing caveat, as you put it, is I will need to dine at a restaurant and write a review about my experience."

"Piece of cake—you've got a ton of those in your diary alone," Sebastian said.

"Well," I said, my voice raised an octave, "it's not that easy. I'm to write a review about *Cristofano Woods*. Getting a table there is impossible."

Saying it aloud made the reality far more gut-wrenching, causing all of the excitement I had stored up to quickly deflate. I remember crashing back down onto the hardwood floor with a sick feeling in my stomach.

"Wait. Hold the freaking phone. Did you just say *Cristofano Woods?*" Sebastian asked with a hint of excitement in his voice.

"Yes." I wondered why he seemed so excited when I felt like shit.

"Baby girl, you must have the best fucking luck in the world." He let out a muffled scream. "We just signed them as a client two weeks ago!"

"You did what?" My heart pounded in excitement. "And wait. Why haven't you told me? You know I've been so wanting to go there since it opened."

"I was planning to take you there in two weeks for your birthday... you know, a sur-prize." He sounded like a circa-1980s valley girl.

I sat up, feeling instantly cured.

"Anyway," Sebastian continued, "when we signed them on as a client, I got a hold of two guest passes. We can totally go tonight if you want."

"Of course I want! What time shall I be ready?" I felt like I had just been awarded a grandiose prize from Publishers Clearing House.

"I'll pick you up at 7," he said. "And wear your black Kate Spade dress and leopard pumps," he added before ending the call.

A little after 8pm that night, a taxi dropped me and Sebastian off in front of *Cristofano Woods*. Even though it was a Wednesday, the place was still poppin' like a popular nightclub. Eager patrons formed a line that wrapped clear around the block. I can't begin to tell you the excitement that poured out of me—I mean, I was about to indulge in one of the hottest new restaurants in New York.

Sebastian led the way toward the entrance doors that were manned by two male greeters. People in line glared at us as we made our way to the front.

"Sorry, the line ends all of the way back there," one greeter told Sebastian, looking him up and down.

"Right, thanks for the info, buddy," Sebastian sarcastically tossed right back. He reached into the interior pocket of his sleek leather jacket and produced a wicked smirk before pulling out the guest passes. "Do these mean anything?"

The greeter glanced at the passes and said, "Yes, of course. Go inside and show those to the hostess, who will gladly seat you."

Once inside, I immediately switched from excited newbie to full-on food critic. I mean I had to in order to be sure I could write an objectively infused, knock-it-the-hell-out-of-the-park review for the interview. Sebastian and I spent at least two hours there that night indulging in the essence of the restaurant's unforgettable uniqueness.

6

Once back home, I stayed up half the night writing and then rewriting what turned out to be—in my opinion—the best fucking wanna-be restaurant review ever.

The day before the interview I shopped for an outfit that screamed 'I am a food critic for a newspaper', after Sebastian lent his fashion expertise.

"This is what you need to look like when you walk into that interview tomorrow," he said as he sipped on a homemade green tea latte. He handed me a page torn out of the latest issue of *Vogue London.*

"This?" I said, feeling somewhat challenged.

"Yep. Don't fight it, sweetie. Trust me. And the model even has your body type and hair style. I'm thinking the outfit alone will get you the job."

I rolled my eyes in protest. "Great, I'll be sure to walk through the doors of *The Hudson News Bee,* fully prepared to call attention to my outfit and leave the review I spent hours crafting, crumpled up in a pitiful ball in the trash bin."

"Put that sarcasm to rest, my dear," he said, shaking his head while sipping his gourmet-style tea latte.

Sebastian had always been about fashion, often dressing better than anyone I had ever known. But he was right about the model. Like me, she was tall, with a slim build, a tiny waist, an ample bosom, and long and wavy reddish-brown hair. She looked fashionably chic in a modern suit that consisted of straight-legged cropped pants, a crisp white button-down blouse that was left tastefully untucked, a matching blazer that seemed to seductively hug her upper body curves, and Penny-Loafer-style shoes that added a twist of old-school elegance.

Admittedly, she looked pretty impressive. But I personally hated everything about suits.

"Sebastian, I'm not too sure about—"

"Hush now," Sebastian interrupted, holding his hand up as if he were dismissing a defiant teenager. "You know I totally know my shit. Now hop on the train and take your cynical butt to the East Village. There is an adorable boutique called Diamonattos. When you walk in, ask for Tonya, and be sure to tell her I sent you. Show her that outfit," he said, pointing to the magazine page. "She'll hook you up. And she better do it for free," he paused and took one last sip of his green tea latte, "'cause the bitch owes me a favor."

Then it finally came.

Friday.

The day of the interview.

I was as nervous as a Black Angus cow at a beef factory. I drank at least five cups of coffee which only intensified the edge more profoundly. I seriously considered taking a shot of tequila but remembered I had sworn off alcohol after some heavy drinking during my freshman year.

Stylishly equipped with a black leather attaché case that protectively held two printed copies of my written review, and smartly dressed in the outfit Sebastian swore would get me the job, I walked into the official headquarters of *The Hudson News Bee* fifteen minutes early. The jittery effects of the caffeine I had consumed earlier had since passed, and I felt relatively calm and collected.

I was greeted by an awfully chipper receptionist who directed me to a waiting room before mentioning someone would be with me soon.

The waiting room was small but had an upbeat appeal with red walls artistically embellished by black and white framed newspaper articles. There were two black sofas and a round glass coffee table that held copies of *Time Magazine* and *The New Yorker*. I was just about to settle down on one of the sofas when a tall, thin man walked into the room.

"Penelope Monroe?" he asked.

"Um, yes." I confirmed.

He approached me and gestured for a hand shake. "Garrett Harrison, food editor for *The Bee*." He smiled.

Meet Garrett Harrison—aka—Mr. Jerkboy, as in the one and only cheating-ass ex-boyfriend. Anyway, allow me to continue...

His smile was extremely infectious, putting me immediately at ease. Not to mention his stellar appearance. He was absolutely gorgeous.

"Pleasure to meet you," I said as I shook his hand. He smelled of Calvin Klein cologne and was dressed extremely casual in Levi's, a blue-and-white striped oxford shirt, and white Vans. I took note of his dark brown eyes as they were somewhat mesmerizing. His short, curly hair was a dirty-blond tone, making him resemble what I envisioned to be the California surfer type, yet his strong New York accent proved otherwise.

"Great, shall we take this to my office?" he asked and motioned for me to follow him. "I'm eager to begin the interview. You're the last candidate," he said as he led me through a room of busy office cubicles.

Once in his office, he invited me to take a seat in one of the two chairs in front of his large mahogany-colored desk where papers and files were haphazardly scattered.

I took a seat, keeping a tight grip on my attaché case that I laid atop my lap. Nerves had definitely crept in.

"So," he began as he slowly rocked back and forth in his squeaky, ergonomically designed, desk chair. "I'm just gonna cut to the chase here. Did you meet your assigned goal? Did you write a review on *Cristofano Woods?*" He annoyingly drummed all ten tips of his fingers on the arms of the chair.

"Of course I did." I was feeling exceptionally proud of my accomplishment. I unzipped the attaché case and removed both copies of the written review and handed them over to him. I was unsure, at this point, why he asked me to bring two printed copies with me.

He nodded and smiled as he took custody of them. "As I mentioned in my email to you, I'm highly impressed. Even more so now because you actually did it—a review of one of the newest restaurants in New York." He leaned in and whispered conspiratorially, "How the fuck did you get into *Cristofano Woods?*"

"With all due respect, Mr. Harrison," I softly cleared my throat before going on, "I value my sources and, as such, can't possibly, under any circumstances, reveal them. I'm sure you, of all people, can understand."

He leaned back into his chair and looked at me with a mystified expression.

Had I gone too far? I anxiously wondered.

He said nothing. At least not verbally. His dark eyes pierced through me like a medieval dagger. He laid one copy on top of his messy desk and handed me the other. "Here, read it aloud, please."

"Um, excuse me? Read it aloud?" I repeated for confirmation. Seemed like a pretty odd request to me.

"Yeah. You see, Miss. Monroe, a good review must sound good when read aloud. So please, indulge me." He leaned back in his chair and continued rocking back and forth, looking as though he had some sort of trick up his sleeve. It was quite intimidating.

"Okay." I nervously cleared my throat and read him my cherished review—aloud.

FOOD DISCLOSURE
by Penelope Monroe

I searched the Internet for impressive synonyms that would artfully convey meanings of the words trendy, unique, succulent, innovative, superb, ultra-chic hip, and magnificent. Those vibrant words collectively define everything that is Cristofano Woods.

Trendy *- the decor. The small, mildly toned-down younger sibling of Marty Raven is a tasteful trendsetter from floor to ceiling.*

Unique *- the food. I mean, yes, it's just pizza, but then again it's not **just** pizza. You'll have to trust me on this one. Hint: it's not the typical-style pizza NY is known for. This is wood-fired pizza. As in baked in real eight-hundred-degree Stefano Ferrara ovens straight outta Naples, Italy. Oh and they also bake their signature pasta and veggie dishes wood-fired style, as well. In fact, everything is wood-fired. Except for their vast selection of wine. But who knows? Maybe that too.*

Succulent *- back to the pizza. I mean a pizza with clams and white sauce? Yup. And every bite of it seemed to seductively melt in my mouth. And*

I've never been one to use the word seductive to define food. But don't simply take my word for it. Go now. Get your own—if you like long lines that wrap around the block. But don't let that stop you. The experience is truly worth the wait.

Innovative - the total concept. Only those Marty Raven *folks could pull this off. What's their secret? If they told us they'd probably have to kill us.*

Superb - the service. Actually it was beyond superb. The team really does know how to woo guests so they'll come back for more and more. And even more. I felt like my waitress was my BFF. In fact, I'm pretty sure she convinced me to name my firstborn after her. Rebecca. Wait. What if my firstborn is a boy?

Ultra-chic hip - the vibe. A place where celebrities and everyday people can playfully dine alike while listening to a diverse selection of loud music.

Magnificent - the experience all summed up. Or perhaps I should have chosen the word magnanimous because the experience as a whole was royally cool.

I didn't want my evening at Cristofano Woods *to come to an end. But all good things must...*

Perhaps I have inspired you to find your indulgence in the magnificently trendy, uniquely succulent, superbly innovative, and ultra-chic hip, hot spot, more famously known as Cristofano Woods.

Cheers to you and yours!

GARRETT LOOKED AT ME STONE-FACED, saying absolutely nothing after hearing what I thought to be a prized review. He stood up, picked up the copy of the review from his desk, and said, "You'll have to excuse me for just one moment." He walked out of his office and closed the door behind him. That moment seemed like an eternity before he returned with another man who had a very obvious receding hairline. He was shorter and much more rounded out than Garrett. He closely resembled an actor from an old 1980s TV show called *Taxi* that Sebastian and I tried to binge watch on Netflix.

I stood up, not knowing exactly what was happening. The rounded-out man held out his hand to shake mine. I nervously wiped the sweat off the palm of my hand onto my pants before going in hard for a firm shake.

"Penelope. Great to meet you. I'm Jake Simms, owner of *The Hudson News Bee.*"

"Oh wow. Good to meet you, Mr. Simms." I smiled generously and instantly remembered the name of the actor I thought he resembled. Danny DeVito...yeah.

"Please, call me Jake," he insisted, "and please, go ahead and sit back down."

I quickly sat back down as instructed.

"Penelope, Garrett showed me your review, and I must say, he and I both think it's excellent work. Print worthy, in fact."

"Print...um, what?" I asked, scratching my head.

"We'd like to run your review," Garrett interjected. "Like now. As in send to print and publish online."

I sat there, unable to speak.

"And we'd like to offer you the position. Full time. Full benefits. Everything. Your writing is phenomenal. Infused with talent," said Jake, as he paced back and forth.

"And the title *Food Disclosure?* Is that something you came up with?" Garrett asked.

I nodded yes.

"It's freaking awesome," said Jake. He approached me, bending down at eye-level, placed his hands on my shoulders, and looked me in the eyes the way my dad used to whenever he wanted to have a heart to heart. "We'd like to give you the opportunity to write a column under that title, every month, at first. Then, if it helps us sell more papers and online subscriptions, you'll eventually write for us every week," he added.

And that, my friends, is how it all began.

I gratefully accepted their offer, signed an employment contract, and *Food Disclosure* launched my career as a food critic. My reviews went from a monthly, to a bi-weekly, and then to a weekly column. I visited and reviewed all types of New York based restaurants— Michelin starred to quaint local bakeries. Just as I hoped, I became known only by name, being careful in keeping my identity concealed. Only the newspaper, family, some college classmates, and Sebastian knew I was *the* Penelope Monroe. Restaurant owners, chefs, and CEOs would religiously read my weekly column, as my written reviews would either make or break them. A good review meant a surge of business. A bad review meant an obvious loss of business, or even a decline in a Chef's overall reputation as in the case of one semi-famous chef and restaurant owner named Jonathan Knight.

Garrett and I began dating about six months after I joined *The Bee's* editorial team. We got serious enough that I assumed he was going to propose. I was so in love with him. Never in my wildest dreams did I expect to find him screwing some stupid bitch in my office.

And now, today, meet the new me: Penelope Monroe, the broken-hearted, unemployed food critic.

Ugh.

I fucking *hate* Mondays.

CHAPTER 2

A cloud of mental clarity hovers over me like a beacon of hope, early the next morning. *Bless you, Tuesday. I simply adore you.*

Thanks to the loft's considerably thin walls, I can hear Sebastian rattling dishes in the kitchen—something he does when trying to entice me out of my bedroom. I managed to avoid him altogether yesterday. Selfishly, I needed the downtime. However, Sebastian is my best friend, and I do owe him a complete account of yesterday's events.

Forcing myself to roll out of bed, I pull my hot-pink satin robe over me, slip into my pink, furry, Powerpuff-girl slippers, and check my reflection in the antique mirror that hangs at a crooked yet complacent angle on the back of my bedroom door. The whites of my eyes are now a blazing red, thanks to the tsunami of tears that flowed down my face last night. And for the record, I'm not, by any means, a crier. But seriously, that shit felt like a rusty crossbow had savagely fractured the heck out of my gullible heart.

Believe me, it hurt. Badly.

But I'm totally over it. *Not really.*

Time to move on to bigger and better things. *Whatever that is.*

As I enter the kitchen, Sebastian greets me with a smile while he stands behind the wide granite breakfast bar, munching on what appears to be a blueberry scone. He has a peculiar obsession with scones—and green tea lattes. He is smartly dressed in black chino pants and a grey pullover sweater that brings out his dark blue eyes. He's always appeared handsome to me; I always seem to gravitate toward the light-haired blue-eyed type. The smile fades off of his cheerful face once he catches a glimpse of the grim expression on mine.

"Oh-My-Freaking-Gosh. What the hell happened to you?" he mumbles, appearing to make a concerted effort not to spit out remnants of scone crumbs everywhere. "You've obviously been crying. What the hell did he do to you?"

Sebastian has never liked Garrett. In fact, he's hated him since the moment I began dating him. The more serious I got with Garrett, the more Sebastian hated him. He referred to him often as the bitchass rat. And now I totally concur, of course.

I morosely drag my furry slipper-covered feet over to the cupboard where we keep our coffee mugs. Out of habit, I grab a mug inscribed *Hudson News Bee*. Ugh.

"Coffee. I am in need of coffee," I mumble pathetically.

Sebastian grabs a hold of my hand and drags me over to one of the barstools. "You better sit. I'll make you some coffee."

I ease onto the barstool and lay my head onto the counter. Seconds later, he places a mug full of coffee in front of me.

"Start talking." He stands behind the breakfast bar counter, arms folded, with a contentious glare in his eyes.

I take a long whiff of the coffee, take a sip, and begin sharing my saga with Sebastian. "Okay, so I went back to the office yesterday evening because I forgot my journal. You know how much I depend on my journal notes."

"Right, I know. But, girlfriend, I have also highly encouraged you to catch up with us Electronic Savvy's and log those journal entries into your iPhone or iPad," Sebastian reprimands, taking a seat in the barstool next to me.

I completely ignore his 'savvy' talk and move on to what's the real issue at hand. "Anyway, I walked into my office only to find Garrett with his editorial assistant."

"Wait. When you say 'with,' do you mean he was—?"

"Yes," I interrupt, covering my ears, not wanting to hear him say it.

"Shit no!"

"Um...yeah. But that's not all," I say, adding even more theatrics to the story.

"And what could possibly top that?"

"He fired me." I begin bawling. Honestly, at this point, I have not decided what part of yesterday hurt the most—the part when I caught Garrett in the act with that slushy chick, or the part when he fired me afterwards.

"Wait. What? He fired you?"

"Yes. Fired. As in, I no longer have a j-o-b. As in, my career? Over."

Sebastian leans in to hug me. "Sweetie, I'm so very sorry this happened to you," he pulls away, seeming to examine my expression, "and yesterday was a Monday of all days too!" He hugs me again. "That freaking bitchass rat can't fire you. I mean you helped make that paper what it is today. Can't you like go to Jake or something?"

"No. Well I mean I probably could go to Jake. But do I really want to? You know, work with Garrett? Besides, Jake is like a father figure to Garrett. Whose side of the boat do you think he'd jump on? Not mine, that's for sure."

"So, what are you going to do, sweetie?"

"I have no clue. But don't worry. As far as rent money goes, you know I'm good—"

"I don't mean what are you gonna do about money, sweetheart," he interrupts. "I mean what are you gonna do...like as in your career? You've worked exclusively for that newspaper ever since you started writing restaurant reviews publicly," he asks, sparking even more uncertainty.

The tsunami of tears makes an unwelcome return.

Sebastian reaches over to grab a hold of my hand. "It's gonna be okay. I mean you are the one and only Penelope Monroe," he assures.

"True. My name is one thing Garrett can't take away from me."

Saying that aloud conjures up an epic idea.

"My page! My followers!" I shout in excitement.

"Honey, if you are thinkin' what I'm thinkin', you better get to work," Sebastian says as he raises himself off the barstool and glances at his teal blue iWatch. "I've gotta run to work, baby girl. Uber is waiting for me outside. You be sure to update me later," he says before kissing me on the forehead. He grabs his keys, briefcase, and a bottle of Perrier out of the fridge before disappearing through the long hallway that leads to the front door. The tumultuous sound of the door slamming is my only confirmation Sebastian has left.

Feeling a rush of confidence come over me, I walk over to the Keurig to brew another cup, then make my way to what used to be the dining room. Sebastian and I creatively converted the space to a home office since we rarely have visitors needing to be entertained in a formal dining room. I turn on my desktop computer as soon as I get to my desk and sit, waiting impatiently for it to boot up Once my home screen pops up, I click the Facebook icon and log on to my *Food Disclosure* page. I click my way through the administrative settings and spitefully delete my ex-boss-friend's access.

You messed with the wrong girl, Garrett Harrison.

You see, I created my Facebook Page when I first started writing reviews for the paper, and it has grown quite the following over the last couple of years—all nine-hundred-thousand, eight-hundred forty-two *Food Disclosure* followers deserve a declarative dose of real disclosure.

JULY 19, 2016

Greetings Foodies!! Thank you all so much for your loyal following and support! You are the best! I wanted to reach out to you all to share some #breakingnews that I want to be sure you hear from me first. As of yesterday, I am no longer a part of #thehudsonnewsbee team. While I can't disclose anything further, I want it known that Penelope Monroe will continue to publish restaurant reviews each week; only those reviews will now come via this Facebook Page. I hope you will continue to follow me as I venture into a new food journey—with you.

More to come later this week...

Cheers to you and yours!

Penelope

ONLY MINUTES after publishing my post, the sought after indicatory likes and comments begin to flood the page. And that's not all. My iPhone blows up with tons of text messages, including one from Jake Simms.

Jake: Good morning...

I immediately reply.

Me: What's up?

Jake: Saw your recent FB post. Can we talk, please?

Me: Talk about what exactly?

Jake: Your employment contract.

Me: Contract? Ok...what about it should we discuss? Thought it was pretty much void since I got fired. You know...a minor technicality.

Jake: Penelope, I don't know exactly what happened, but I don't want to lose the weekly column.

Me: Right. And I can't ever work with Garrett again. Not after what occurred yesterday.

Jake: So are you resigning? Because you're not fired.

I stare at his response, feeling my blood begin to boil.

Me: I was definitely fired yesterday—was even told to clear out my office and everything.

Jake: Can you come to my office today? We can work this out.

Me: Okay. I'll be there in an hour.

Do I really want to show my face there? Nope.

A little over an hour later I stand here in the booming lobby of *The Hudson News Bee* headquarters in front of the huge double-doored elevators. I can see my reflection glaze through the glossy chrome-plated doors that repeatedly open and close; I'm unable to muster up the courage needed to actually step onto the elevator and ride up to the twelfth floor. I have just about convinced myself to leave—hurry back to the sanctity of home, but realize I must do this. The elevator doors slide open. It's her. The salty floozy I caught Garrett with yesterday who has the nerve, by the way, to brazenly look me up and down as she slithers past me.

Now, there's all the courage you need.

Infuriated, I stomp onto the elevator, armed with uninhibited emotion, push button twelve, and before I know it, I storm into Jake's office.

"Penelope," Jake rises up from his desk chair, "glad you made it in."

"Right. So, why did you want me to come in today?" I slide into the chair closest to the door, cleverly outlining my escape plan.

"Yes. Um, well I finally got Garrett to cough up what the hell happened between you two yesterday."

"Uh-huh," I manage.

"And uh, well I'm truly sorry he fired you. His behavior was completely unacceptable."

I offer a firm nod in agreement.

"On behalf of the paper, I want to assure you, you're not *really* fired. He had no sustainable grounds to terminate you."

"Okay. So what does that mean, exactly?"

"It means you can continue working here. *I* want you to continue working here."

"But like I said in my text message, I can't work with Garrett."

"Look, Penelope, you know Garrett is like a son to me. I can't fire him simply because you caught him cheating."

Simply because? "Then I guess we are done here." I get up, grateful I'm only a step away from the door.

"Wait!" He rushes to the door. "It's your contract, Penelope."

"Void. Fired. Remember?"

"There's a clause."

"I am fully aware of confidentiality constraints. I know what I can and cannot share."

"No. There is more than the confidentiality agreement."

I close the door and sit back down. "What do you mean?"

Jake retrieves a file from his file cabinet and hands it to me. "Look inside. Page three. Paragraph twelve. I highlighted it for you." His voice is subdued and shaky instead of its usually vivid baritone.

I copiously peruse over the highlighted paragraph.

'ANYTHING CREATED *by the employee for the company belongs to the company. The title "Food Disclosure" was developed by the contracted employee prior to employment contract development. However, it was agreed upon by employee and* Hudson News Bee *to utilize the title "Food Disclosure" upon commencement of employment. In the event the contracted employee and* Hudson News Bee *terminate employment contract, by any means,* Hudson News Bee *can continue the use of the title "Food Disclosure" by the agreed monetary purchase amount of $250,000. After which, contracted employee no longer has rights to use the title "Food Disclosure" with a competitive newspaper, magazine, blog, or any other social media outlet.'*

UNCERTAINTY CAUSES me to read the clause again. Admittedly, I didn't read this part of the contract when I was hired two years ago; I was most likely too excited.

"So this means, if I leave, I can't take *Food Disclosure* with me? But it's *my* creation."

Jake shrugs his shoulders, and I can't decide if the expression on his heavily wrinkled face is of bitter dismay or of bitter excitement.

"Right," I scoff in the discovery of an epiphany, "this is about my Facebook post this morning. I posted it under the Food Disclosure Page."

Jake nods in silence.

"So, now what? Are you gonna sue me since I inadvertently published a post under that name?"

"No, Penelope. My goal is to keep you on board, not to sue you."

He sits on the edge of the desk with his arms folded, seeming to wait for my response.

And when I offer no reply, he finally continues.

"But clearly you don't wish to work here anymore. I was afraid of that." Jake walks around his desk, opens the top drawer, and removes three envelopes. "If you're seriously not staying with the Bee, I'm obligated to allow you out of your contract due to the circumstances. Inside of these envelopes are items that may be of great interest to you. One contains a check for the money we owe you for this pay period plus accrued vacation time. Another has a letter of recommendation, which I feel more than obliged to give you given the course of unsatisfactory events that has led us here today. And one contains a check in the amount of two hundred and fifty-thousand dollars, for the purchase of the name *Food Disclosure*." Jake holds up each envelope, brandishing them like one would three gold medals.

Without the slightest bit of hesitation, I grab the envelopes, deciding to leave the newspaper with my name, dignity, and a respectable amount of money to boot.

At once, a surge of anxiety builds up, making me feel as though this building is going to suffocate me. Waiting for the elevator can't possibly get me out quickly enough. I run down the twelve flights of stairs as if my total existence depends on it. Once on the ground floor, I shove the exit door open, stumble onto the busy sidewalk, and desperately breathe in the smog-filled New York City air. I gratefully take in the bewitching essence of freedom and notice a touristy couple walk past me, both holding a small to-go bag from *Cristofano Woods*.

The irony makes me smile and an unexpected urge to bid *Hudson News Bee* a proper farewell pours over me. I pivot to face the building and eloquently present a much-deserved one finger salute. Here's to bigger and better things.

CHAPTER 3

I roam down bustling Fifth Avenue, lost in a pitiful satire of reflection.

What the hell are you gonna do now? I mean, really? You've got no boyfriend and no job.

While quite annoying, my flustered introspection makes me realize I've never truly considered not working for the newspaper. Not having a boyfriend? Who the hell even cares? Single is the new Prada; anyone who can afford it seemingly flaunts it with this sort of blatant swag. I've got swag—*I think.* And if I've learned anything from watching *How To Be Single*, it's best to embrace my new-found status for as long as I can.

My thoughts are interrupted by the sounds of New York: whooshing city buses, blaring car horns, and the ear-piercing scream of a NY City cop's whistle. Watching him perform an animated dance directing traffic in the middle of a pothole-infested road causes me to snicker in amusement. A quick glance at the street sign above reveals I've walked at least three blocks, landing on West Forty-Sixth Street and Eighth Avenue. Old habits really do die hard. I mean why wouldn't a natural-born food critic be drawn to Restaurant Row? A dedicated stretch of New York's finest eateries, as described in some article I read online. Finest? Well...I suppose most of them are.

Amid a pity-party-induced trance and an all too predictable force of habit, I step into FlashBurger. Sebastian always says, "Everyone needs a good burger when they're having a shitty day or a celebratory day." Obviously, I'm here to memorialize my shittybratory day.

I've eaten here plenty of times, yet have never written a review. Oddly, Garrett had something against the newspaper reviewing 'burger joints'. *Pompous little grinch.*

Once I'm seated, I order a Bonfire Burger and fries, then whip out my iPhone to text Sebastian.

Me: Met with Jake. News to share when you're free.

Sebastian: WTF woman? I'm so gonna FaceTime you right now.

One second later, Sebastian's face is electronically embedded onto the screen of my iPhone.

"Hey," I say, welcoming his flashy expression.

"I've got 15 mins to get the 411, so spill the coffee beans, please." Sebastian pats his blond, spiky crown, appearing to idolize his own image on the screen. "Wait, are you where I think you are?"

"Yep. FlashBurger."

"Please tell me you're about to indulge the hell out of a juicy cut of beef based on pure celebratory reasons? I'm so freaking jealous right now."

"More like a shittybratory event, you know—shitty plus celebratory?" I explain.

"You're so comical at times. Okay. Talk to me."

"So, after you left this morning, I posted on the Food Disclosure Facebook Page," I begin, as a perky waitress delivers my food.

"I know, I read it while en route to the office. You know I get those wonderful notifications each time you post." He smiles wryly.

"Okay. Well, immediately after the post, Jake sent me a text. And in an effort to make this part of the story short, he asked me to the office for a meeting." I swirl a few fries in ketchup and effortlessly cram them into my mouth. Sebastian's eyes widen, colorfully illustrating his amusement. Although, I can't make out if he's reacting to my eating antics or to my story.

"So," I take a sip of water and continue, "I made my way to the office, only for him to try to get me to stay. When he realized I was clearly ready to just move on, he brought up some clause in the contract I signed two years ago." I remove the top bun from the burger before taking a bite—gotta stay away from carbs to remain fit if I'm gonna own my newly appointed station as 'single girl.'

"Um, what clause?"

"Right. Apparently I signed a stipulation of payment for the name *Food Disclosure* in the event the employment contract comes to an end."

"Please, honey," he shakes his head and massages his temple, "you've gotta break it down into legal shit for dummies jargon. You know I get brain freeze when I think too hard."

Sebastian's timely theatrics make me giggle. "Basically, I agreed to sell my rights to *Food Disclosure* upon termination of my employment contract. No longer am I able to use that name for anything, including social media, blogs, you name it. It's all theirs now," I explain, suddenly losing my appetite.

"So how much did those trolls pay you for your valuable commodity?"

I dig into my bag. "Two-hundred and fifty-thousand dollars." I grin, holding up the check to the iPhone screen.

"Oooh la la! One quarter of a mil? No wonder you're having a whatever-bratory meal." He claps his hands in excitement.

"It's shittybratory," I correct even though I know he's being his cynical self. "Shitty to actually leave the newspaper, yet celebratory because I didn't leave empty-handed. My name, dignity, and a decent amount of dinero walked out of *Hudson News Bee* in one piece." Instinctively, I place the check back into my bag when the waitress comes to remove my plate from the table.

"Congrats, baby girl," says Sebastian. "I'll make us a couple of commemorative cocktails when I get home this evening. I'm thinking some fruity cosmopolitans are in order. So, are you like gonna rename that page?"

"Yep, sure am. Just as soon as I can conjure up something catchy to call it."

"Better be quick, my dear. My guess is they've paid you for the name and are probably expecting you to abide by the agreement. Do you have your MacBook?"

"Um, of course I do. To me, a MacBook is like the new old slogan for American Express: Don't Leave Home Without It," I say, in an unsuccessful attempt at being witty.

Sebastian rolls his eyes. "Uh, yeah…I'm gonna totally purge that comment from my memory. Anyway, open up that laptop and get to work on a new name. I don't want to hear about you getting sued by those bitchass dirtbags. Anyhow, I've really gotta run now. Some chef wants our representation and we are meeting in two minutes and thirty seconds. Tootles." Sebastian blows me a kiss before ending our FaceTime session. He's right, you know. I need to access that page and remove the *Food Disclosure* name. But what do I call it?

I ask the waitress for a cup of coffee (aka thinking serum) and pull out my MacBook. The post from this morning has now reached over eighty-thousand likes. And the comments? Endless.

One says:

Penelope you are the best! So looking forward to your next journey. Don't stop informing us where to eat. We depend on you!!

And another says:

Penelope Monroe, I only read The Hudson News Bee *once a week—for* **your** *review! Please keep posting. Love ya!*

There are lots more and all give me much-needed peace of mind. Perhaps I can do this on my own? Who needs an overtly stilted periodical anyway? Not me.

The waitress brings me a hot cup of coffee. "Brewed a fresh pot for you," she says and smiles. "Would you mind if I leave the bill with you now? I'm going on a break soon."

"Uh, no. I don't mind at all." I smile, thinking I owe this place a review—a good one. Wait! The exact thought of giving FlashBurger a good review invokes a pretty conceivable notion; only I can't dial it in without a helping hand from Sebastian. Between the two of us, he's the visionary architect.

I send him a quick text message.

Me: Hey, I've got an idea that needs your creative expertise. See you later at home?

I sit staring anxiously at my phone, awaiting a reply.

Sebastian: Yes! Brainstorming session!! And we can totally do this with our cosmo bevs in hand. Oooh, we can order Indian takeout too. Feeling super excited! Catch ya later, babe. Oh, and by the way, I totally need your help with a project. I'll fill you in tonight. xo

Help with a project? Sebastian is skilled at ending our text message convo's with a cliffhanger—he appropriately calls them text-hangers. And now, as he probably predicted, I can't help but ponder the kind of project he needs my help with.

I pack up, pay for my scrumptious burger, and make my way toward the jam-packed NY Subway station. Thanks to Jake Simms and his generous payment for *Food Disclosure*, I now have to make a dreaded run to the bank before going home. While most would be beyond thrilled about receiving an extra $250,000 buckaroos, I'm not. Not really, anyway. Why? That's a subject I've been able to masterfully evade at all costs… Well at least so far, anyway.

CHAPTER 4

*W*infield Bank and Trust is owned and operated by the Winfield family, a semi-aristocratic bunch, well known for real-estate investments and venture capitalism. I've known the family for what feels like ages, as my parents and Mr. Winfield served twenty years together in the military. Gracie, the youngest Winfield, was at NYU with me, however, she abruptly disappeared junior year. Rumor has it, she spent the majority of her time drinking at frat parties and subsequently failed all of her courses (except for the swanky Fashion Couture 101 online course). Anyway, justly disgusted with her reckless behavior and concerned about the possible blemish to the family name, Mr. Winfield apparently yanked Gracie out of NYU and shoved her deep into the nuts and bolts of the family banking business. Since then, she's been sort of managing the Winfield Bank branch close to my Harlem loft.

Only seconds after I walk through the branch's gold-trimmed doors, Gracie greets me with an erratic wave.

"Penelope! Great to see you!" Outfitted in a bronze tight-fitting pencil skirt, a fuchsia cashmere button-down sweater, and black stilettos, she approaches me with a jovial grin. Her ensemble reminds me of something the character Rizzo from the movie *Grease* would wear.

"We haven't seen you in quite some time now. How are you?" The tone of her voice drags on as if she's training to be some kind of debutant.

"I'm okay. Just here to deposit a couple of checks." I take a quick look around and notice the extensive queue of customers.

"Oh, of course! I can certainly assist you with that. Just come on over to my desk and have a seat." She sort of bounces as she takes the lead to her desk at the far end of the bank.

"Thanks Gracie." I stifle a giggle, trying hard not to offend her.

"Oh, it's always a pleasure!" She gestures for me to take a seat in one of the high-back chairs, sits down, and types on her desktop computer. Her long ruby-colored acrylic nails perform an exuberant tap dance across the keyboard as if in desperate need of attention. "Just give me a quick second to pull up your account. Uh yes, here we go. You mentioned a deposit?"

"Yes," I gratefully give her the checks, feeling relieved to rid my hands of them.

Gracie browses over each check, looks at me briefly through her blue-framed Coach eyeglass lenses, and produces a half-cranked grin. Using a fancy electronic calculator, she tallies both checks and promptly processes them for deposit.

I nervously tap the tip of my shoe against the chair leg. To be honest, banks really aren't my thing.

"Will you need anything else today?"

"Nope. Just the deposits, please." My heart begins to sprint.

"Okay then. Just let me grab your statement from the printer and you'll be all set."

Gracie jaunts over to the printer and returns with my bank statement, but takes a seat again before handing it it me.

Please, just please, give it to me so I can be on my merry little way. I place my hand over my chest to keep my racing heart from jumping out.

"Penelope, are you sure you don't wish to make any changes to your account?"

Oh goodness. Here she goes.

"I'd be more than happy to set up a market rate account for you," she continues, "or even a simple investment account which will allow your funds to grow."

There is a brief pause as she nervously fumbles with the keyboard. "As of now, the money is just sitting there—doing absolutely nothing for you." Her tone sounds patronizing, however, I know she means well. At least the expression on her extensively made-up face suggests she's sympathetic. It's the same furrowed-brow look she produces each time she consults on my money management.

"No thank you, Gracie. I'm happy with my account the way it is." I extend my hand—an obvious reach for my bank statement.

"Of course." She politely smiles, shakes her head as if disappointed, and finally hands me my statement. "Just let me know when you're ready to make changes."

After thanking Gracie for her help, I make a mad dash through the bank's double doors, pleased to have successfully averted the chronic panic attack I usually get during every dire trip to the bank.

I take a few steps away from the bank and lean against the cool concrete wall of the coffee shop next door. *Get a hold of yourself. When are you going to be able to walk into the bank and not freak out?*

Taking in the soothing breaths my crafty yoga instructor models, I brace myself and peek at the statement.

Balance: $2,559,789.08

Yep. It's all there. *Still.* Thanks to Mom and Dad—a melancholy reminder of their eternal absence.

* * *

"Hun, what's the name of that Indian restaurant we order our takeout from? My overindulgent palate is longing for some of their Chicken Tikki Masala—mainly that damn sauce. It's like heaven on a freaking plate. Or hell on a plate, depending on how spicy they make it."

Sebastian is in the kitchen mixing our shittybratory cosmopolitans as I sprawl gloomily on the couch in the living room.

"*Mazaydar*," I shout in reply.

I have been in this same spot since my return home from the bank this afternoon and seriously doubt Sebastian has noticed my somber mood. He's been talking nonstop since he arrived home a little over an hour after I did. First, he mumbled something about the Uber driver's "hot-licious" face. Then, a trivial mention of setting aside time to shop for shoes, followed by a smug remark about me needing to update my "drab" wardrobe to reflect my newly single status.

"Yes, *Mazaydar*! I'm gonna call and place an order. Want some of that curry chicken you always get?" He appears from the kitchen holding two cosmopolitans in the silver-rimmed cocktail glasses we won on a Caribbean cruise with his younger sister Hannah three years ago. With care, he places my drink onto the oval coffee table and switches on the floor lamp. The bright light gleams upon my face like I'm under some type of vehement interrogation.

"Sure," I grumble from underneath the fringed pillow where my head is now appropriately buried.

"Honey…are you okay?" Sebastian removes the pillow and looks at me with a bewildered expression.

"Me? Okay?" I sit up and take a hearty sip of the fruity drink. "Not really." I lie back down and squeeze my eyes shut. "I went to the bank earlier today."

Sebastian drops into the oversized chair adjacent to the couch and conveys nothing verbally—his silence alone speaks volumes, offering an empathetic gaze—the sort of empathy only a true BFF can adequately provide.

A trip to the bank always leaves me feeling solemn for hours—or sometimes even days afterward, bringing back to mind the ugly truth that my parents are no longer alive. They were abruptly taken from me a year ago by a truck driver who fell asleep at the wheel. As an only child, Mom and Dad meant everything to me. Their untimely demise still hurts. And that money—a combination of funds from a life insurance policy and a settlement from the truck company that employed the driver who took them away from me—is a dismal and harsh reminder.

"Oh Penelope, I am so sorry. You should have waited and I would have gone with you in a heartbeat." Sebastian reaches over and grabs my hand. "I know how much you hate the bank. Was Gracie there?"

"Yep, but she didn't bully me too much this time. She only tried once to get me to place the money into some type of money-market account."

"Well, as much as I hate adding alcohol to an abrasive wound, you know Gracie's right. If you're not sure what to do with all of that money you should at least—"

"How about we just order our Indian takeout and discuss this another time...or never," I keenly interject. I know Sebastian means well, but really? I'd much rather walk around naked in Times Square, in the snow, than discuss this right now.

"Sure thing, babe. Food makes everything better. I'm totally starving anyway. We worked our asses off straight through lunch today, and frankly, I'm surprised I'm even alive." He fans his face as if he's trying to avoid passing out.

As usual, Sebastian's excessive dramatics makes me giggle. He calls *Mazaydor* and places our takeout order as I chug the fruity cosmo, hoping the magical drink brings a sense of calm to my overactive nerves.

"Food should be here in about twenty-five minutes, doll face." He looks at my empty glass, "Would you care for another?"

"That would be lovely, thank you."

Before long, Sebastian and I are lounging in the living room, indulging in the essence of fine Indian takeout, zippy cosmos, and Madonna's Greatest Hits CD playing softly in the background. Sebastian's choice, of course.

"So, what exactly do you need my help with?" I ask Sebastian, recalling his earlier text-hanger.

"Uh, no." He waves his finger in protest. "You go first—your last text mentioned you have an idea that needs my creative expertise. Better speak about that now before I finish this drink off," he says,

31

taking a small sip of his drink. "We've so gotta channel this beautiful mind now...while I'm still coherent."

I chuckle in response. "Okay, so yeah, I had this epic idea of what I can turn my Food Disclosure Page to."

Sebastian raises his eyebrows, displaying his curiosity.

"What do you think of me writing only good restaurant reviews?" I clap my hands and smile, feeling utterly impressed.

"Go on..." Sebastian says, taking a bite of the spicy chicken marsala.

"Okay, so I would use the Facebook page to post only positive reviews."

"Hmm. Sounds good, but like how often do you plan to do this? I mean post?"

"Um, daily?"

"Really? Every freaking single day? Honey, won't that be kinda hard to pull off? That is three-hundred and sixty five days—we are talking rain, snow, wind, or shine."

"Right," I say, feeling a tad deflated. "Well, this is obviously why I need *your* inventive assistance. I suck at this." I sit with my arms folded, pouting pathetically.

Sebastian's eyes sparkle with pensive thoughtfulness as his creative juices brew. He finishes off his plate of Indian takeout and this, of course, prompts me to take this time-out to eat more of my savory curry chicken.

Suddenly, as though whomped with clarity from his *Conception God*, Sebastian shares his eureka moment. "Oh yeah, I've got it now! And you, my dear, are so gonna love it." He stands up as if he is about to anoint me with prolific words of wisdom.

Immediately, I put my plate down and swallow a mouthful of rice, giving 'Sebastian the Great' my full and undivided attention.

"To expand on your idea of posting only good reviews, how about you post only once a week—not every single day—on a Monday?"

I feel my mouth open wide about to share my blooming discontent, only to be quickly interrupted.

"Now before you go off at the mouth like a feisty chihuahua, barking about how much you hate Mondays and *refuse* to do anything work related on that day, blah, blah, blah, blah, blah—please allow me to finish."

I nod, trying to picture myself looking like a feisty chihuahua. *Is that what I really look like when I am upset?* But Sebastian knows, for years, I haven't liked working on a Monday—given how much I truly dislike that day of the week. At times, I've gladly worked a Saturday or Sunday instead.

"Anyway," he rolls his eyes and continues, "your weekly posts will create this sort of buzz in the restaurant world centered completely around you—Penelope Monroe—and your merited area of expertise." He begins to pace back and forth, his arm waving in the air, adding to the theatrics like a timed sequence of special effects. "For your fans it will be a paradigm of where to eat." He pauses to take a sip of his cosmo. "And for chefs and restaurant owners, your weekly chronicle will be a Golden Ticket they'll all be competing for—because every restaurant will crave your honorable mention." He takes a deep breath and wipes a small bead of sweat off of his forehead as if sharing his epiphany was all too exhausting.

I sit motionless, taking it all in. I mean, I knew calling on Sebastian for help would be essential, but this idea, to me, is beyond epic. It's colossal, except for the *Monday* part.

"Sebastian, I love it, love it, love it, looove it!" I jump up and give him a hug. "But why did you say every Monday?"

"Honey, you're not the only person in this world who hates Mondays. So why not turn Monday into a good day by sharing a good review?"

"Okay, that makes sense, but what do I name it?"

"Name what?"

"The Facebook page. I can't call it Food Disclosure anymore."

"Oh yeah, right. I got so carried away I forgot to mention that. Why don't you name it The Fifty-Two Week Chronicles?" Sebastian's voice begins to slur as he finishes the last sip of his cosmo and crashes down onto the couch. He is a bit of a lightweight.

"The Fifty-Two Week Chronicles?" I repeat, deciding it does have a nice ring to it.

"Yep. There are fifty-two Mondays in a year, and *your* page will be a chronicled source of viable restaurant information for foodies and restauranteurs alike." He stifles a yawn and positions his head on top of the fringed pillow.

I ponder his prime advice and decide it makes total sense.

"Thanks so much, Sebastian, I really don't know what I'd do without you. You're the best." I lean over and kiss him on the cheek.

His eyes look a little heavy as if it's a struggle to stay awake.

"Sebastian, before you drift off to dreamland, please let me know what you meant in your text message."

"What do you mean?"

"You left me hanging with a text that said you totally need my help with a project."

"Oh yeah, that." He yawns and curls up like a sleepy little lion cub. "A chef came in today seeking the PR Firm's help rebuilding his restaurant's image. I was thinking, since you have some free time on your hands, you can totally work for the firm as a restaurant consultant to help him bring his restaurant stats up to par."

Seconds later, and I really do mean *seconds* later, Sebastian slips into a deep-ass coma and leaves me—once again—with a buzz-killing cliff-hanger.

CHAPTER 5

*W*aking up to the humming sound of a blender after having a sleepless night is beyond uncool. Especially when my head is pounding. But it's not what you think. I don't have a throbbing hangover. I am, however, recovering from a God-awful nightmare. And I'm talking *A Nightmare On Elm Street* level nightmare. You see, I had this bizarrely frightening dream that Sebastian said he volunteered *me*, of all the people in the fucking universe, to work for his PR Firm as a restaurant consultant. I mean really—has anyone ever heard of a fired food critic turned restaurant consultant? Yet, it could be worse. I mean if the nightmare wasn't actually a nightmare, but instead, you know, like *real*?

The humming sound coming from the kitchen has intensified and is now accompanied by—singing? *Is that Sebastian?*

I jump out of bed with only one mission in mind: *make the freaking noise stop.*

With all intents and purposes, I march down the hall straight to the kitchen, covering my ears the whole way, shielding them from what I guess poor Sebastian believes is singing. *'You must be my lucky star, cause you shine on me wherever you are'*… Madonna could actually sue him for false impersonation.

Sebastian stands in front of the blender as it whirls away, his ears outfitted with red Beats headphones, and his eyes closed, as he emphatically rocks out. I can't help but giggle. I stare in awe, immobilized—just for a minute—tempted to make a run back to my room, grab my tablet, and record this YouTube-able moment. However, my headache beseechingly reminds me of its desperate call to action: *make the freaking noise stop—now!*

"Sebastian, please!" I shout realizing, 1) he can't hear me or see me, and 2) my *own* shouting has worsened my headache.

After I stomp around the counter and over to the blender to shut it off myself, Sebastian looks at me stupefied.

"Oh, you're awake now." He removes the headphones from over his ears and positions them around his neck as if wearing headphones around one's neck is the new fashion craze.

I decide a simple eye-roll is an extraordinarily sufficient reply.

The kitchen counter is spattered with all sorts of fruit and vegetable peelings: cucumbers, oranges, mangoes, bananas, green apples, and carrots. Sebastian's famous hangover smoothie.

"Would you care for a Hangover Smoothie?" Sebastian asks, as if on cue, pouring some of the olive-green colored beverage into a glass.

"No thank you. I'm just gonna settle for some coffee...and some Tylenol."

"Sweetie, you look like crap. Perhaps you *should* have some of this invigorating smoothie. It's like a miracle worker. I promise you, this stuff here will make your hangover nonexistent." He takes a meaningful gulp before placing the glass on the counter and begins to clean up the fruit and vegetable peelings.

"Well, I don't have a hangover. I just couldn't sleep after having a horrible dream. A nightmare actually." I take my cup of coffee and plop down onto the barstool.

"Oh, do tell. I can look it up on that online dream encyclopedia website. I once had a dream I was being chased by a freaking koala bear. Of course I looked that shit up right away for analysis. Wanna know what it said?"

"Um...okay." I say, knowing quite well that I'm going to hear about it anyway.

"Well, there were two meanings from two different websites. One said dreaming of a koala symbolizes love and friendship. The other site said dreaming of running from a bear means I am fearful. So I just combined the two and figured I was running from love and friendship."

I laugh internally. "And were you? Running from love and friendship?"

"Oh, goodness no. Well, wait." He pauses and appears to resort to deep thought for a few seconds. "There was this guy in my class that kept asking me out, but he was not at all my type. Too short. Anyway I guess I was running from his advances."

"And did the analysis of the dream make you change your mind about that guy and go out with him?"

"Uh, no. Analysis or not, he was still way too short for me."

I scratch my head, feeling completely unfulfilled by that story.

Sebastian finishes cleaning, grabs his miracle drink, and sits down next to me.

"But seriously. Tell me about this dream that kept you up all night."

"Okay. I had a frightening dream that you volunteered me to work for your PR Firm. As some sort of restaurant consultant." I pause, taking a sip of coffee, "Working with some chef."

Sebastian surveys me with a dumbfounded expression. "You're kidding, right?" He positions his hand on my forehead as if to assess my temperature.

I shake my head. "No."

"A frightening dream?" He places his fingers over his mouth as if he needs to stifle his words. "Honey, you really do need some of this smoothie. That was not at all a *dream*. It was totally real shit."

"Stop toying with me, Sebastian. It was a dream."

"I'm not *toying.* " His tone, severely patronizing. "Okay you may have had too many cosmos last night so let me explain." He walks over to the cupboard, grabs a glass, pours some of the smoothie, and slides the glass over to me. *Yum.*

"So yesterday, a chef came into the firm seeking representation. He said an unfortunate occurrence caused a setback to the business and its image. We've never taken on a chef, so we agreed it would be great for the firm. I thought of you right away. I mean you're *you* and you know a great deal about food and restaurant etiquette...etcetera."

Of course all I can do is sit here rocking side to side on the wobbly barstool, as I clearly suffer from inaudible shock. Did he just seriously confirm he *did* indeed volunteer me? Oh, wait, I get it. This is part of the nightmare. Obviously I'm still sleeping. Duh.

"So will you do it?" Sebastian's voice blatantly affirms I'm not at all still sleeping. Damn.

"And what makes you so sure I can do this? I've never worked at a restaurant."

He sits back down beside me with a heedful expression. "Um, yeah. Well, the way I see it, you know how a restaurant should be from the decor, to the service, and, of course, the food. You're perfect. Please, Penelope. It will help the firm...me out."

I sip on more coffee and think for just a bit. I mean I guess I can help Sebastian out. What harm can it do? Besides he's my BFF, and I wouldn't be doing my part if I didn't help a friend in need. He's certainly come to my aid.

Several times.

"Ok. I'll do it."

Sebastian practically leaps off the barstool to give me an enormous hug. "Thank you, thank you, thank you!"

"You're welcome! Only wait," I say, suddenly struck with an awful thought.

"Oh no...what?"

"Well, we know my identity as Penelope Monroe has only been restricted to my restaurant reviews. The public eye does not know me."

"Yep. Thought about that already and you'll have to go in under a clever disguise. It will be fun actually."

"A clever disguise?"

"Yes. Totally. You can choose a more suitable name and even..." he looks me up and down, "update your wardrobe. Maybe even add some smart-looking eyeglasses to make you look more consultant-like. But leave the wardrobe stuff up to me." He walks over to the blender, rinses it out, places it on the dish rack to dry, then looks at his watch. "I've gotta go before I'm late for work. Thanks again for agreeing to do this for me. It's gonna be so much fun! Take time today to think of a new name."

"Um, I've already got one."

"You do?"

"Kennedy Prescott," I say, feeling proud.

"Kennedy Prescott?" He snickers as he grabs his messenger bag, keys, and a bottle of Perrier out of the fridge. "It's quite fitting."

"I think it has a restaurant-consultant-like vibe to it. I once knew a girl with that name, in the third grade. Back then I wanted to be her. And now I can. At least by name anyway."

It's true, when I was in the third grade, we lived in California while Mom and Dad were stationed at Los Angeles Air Force Base. We rented a lovely home and I attended a school in Pacific Palisades. In my class was a popular girl—Kennedy Prescott—who seemed to be perfect. I loved that name. Truthfully, I've been secretly using the name Kennedy Prescott as my cover when I book restaurant reservations. And once, I looked up the *real* Kennedy Prescott on Facebook and she's still as classy as she was back in the third grade. A successful interior designer, married to a handsome successful lawyer. In other words, still perfect.

"You're pretty funny...Kennedy." He winks at me then heads down the hall to leave.

"Um, Sebastian?" I yell after him.

"Yes?" he replies off in the distance.

"What's the name of the chef I will be working with?"

There is a brief pause that makes me suspect Sebastian has left. But I didn't hear the door slam closed as he annoyingly allows every single time he leaves the loft.

"Um yeah," he yells from the distance, "the chef's name is Jonathan Knight."

The sound of the door shutting closed startles me. Or possibly it's a combination of the sound of the door and the words that came out of Sebastian's mouth. Jonathan Knight. Part of me wants to run down the hall, open the door, and read Sebastian the Riot Act. Only that part of me is being held hostage by the part who looks at her iPhone and figures it's just as easy to send a text message.

So I take another sip of coffee, grab my iPhone, and calmly resort to sending Sebastian the following text message:

Me: What the fuck?

He immediately replies.

Sebastian: What the fuck, what?

Me: Jonathan Freaking Knight?

Sebastian: Wait. His middle name isn't really 'Freaking', is it?

I ignore his mockery and continue to focus on the facts.

Me: You do realize who he is?

Sebastian: Yes. But it's going to be okay.

Me: How can it be okay? I supposedly ruined his restaurant with my review. The review he totally deserved. You know he totally hates me, right?

Sebastian: Right. But he won't know it's you because you won't be you. You'll be Jackie Kennedy. Or whoever.

He added a smiley face emoji for effect.

Me: It's Kennedy Prescott. And you're really not helping, by the way.

Sebastian: Woman, please calm the hell down. Anyway, they say the best way to get over a man is to get a new one.

Me: ????

I have no idea what the hell Sebastian means. And who the hell is this *they* people always quote? *They* say this. *They* say that. Blah, blah blah.

Sebastian: Well, I figure the same applies to a job. To get over one, you need to get a new one. Besides, Jonathan is fucking hotttt. You may very well be able to kill two birdies with one stone. You'll get over being fired by working as a restaurant consultant for *Manifique*.

THE FIFTY-TWO WEEK CHRONICLES

And if you and Jonathan hit it off, you can get over getting dumped too.

Me: Yeah, only I wasn't dumped. Garrett cheated on me, remember?

Sebastian: Tomato / Tamahto.

I reply with a thumbs up emoji, which for me doesn't simply mean *okay*.

It literally means *fuck off*.

CHAPTER 6

On my way to yoga I've only now realized I have never just sat here and observed. For the past couple of years, I've stepped onto this very train, five days a week, with my head literally buried in my iPhone or MacBook, browsing online copies of restaurant reviews: blogs, newspapers, magazines—wherever a review could be read. You see, it would have been extremely taboo to publish an opinion of a restaurant during the same week another critic published one about the same restaurant. I suppose it's also worth mentioning I was—and still am—a super fangirl of Mr. Gregory Hambrick, an extremely famous food critic here in New York who writes a restaurant review column for a well-known newspaper. I aspired to be just like him. Well not like him personally, but I wanted to emulate his writing style and became pretty obsessed with his reviews—more so after he mentioned me in one of his articles. Well, he *kind* of mentioned me. Okay, fine. I admit, I'm not entirely certain. But to this day, I highly suspect he did. Mr. Hambrick wrote the article, in question, five days after *The Hudson News Bee* published my very first review. I remember sitting on the A-Train on my way to work when I read Mr. Hambrick's review. I was quite taken aback when I got to the end of the article. *There seems to be new girl in town who, apparently,*

writes for a rival newspaper. While she knows her stuff in the area of food, she obviously lacks taste in employers. Truthfully, I wish we could have snagged her first. PM, if you're reading this, be sure to look me up—that is, of course, when you decide you are ready to write for a real newspaper.

PM—as in Penelope Monroe? Yep, I was pretty confident he was speaking about me. I took a screenshot and sent it via text message to Sebastian who totally concurred and insisted I pick up a print copy to hold onto as a keepsake. I jumped off the train one stop early and grabbed two copies from the newsstand. Once at work, I cut out the article from one of the copies and hung it up on my very tiny, very bare, cubicle wall. I stared at it in awe for a good fifteen minutes. Alright, it was actually about thirty minutes. Then, I gleefully showed the other copy to Garrett just before we entered an editorial meeting. He scoffed when I implied the snippet was about me (he was quite the bitchass). But, I ignored him and made a personal vow to ask Mr. Gregory Hambrick if that was indeed meant for me. I mean, of course, if and when I'm ever lucky enough to meet him. And if I'm not too busy recovering from passing out like all fangirls do.

So today, for the first time in two years, I'm able to sit here and finally do it. People watch. My copious observations are catastrophically mind-blowing: almost everyone has their own heads buried in some sort of electronic device. Anyway, on account of modern technology, people watching is now officially boring. And borderline creepy—thanks to *The Girl On The Train*.

The train comes to a stop and the accordion style doors open in unison. Like clockwork, NY City commuters rush past me, hop off the train, take a swift jog up the staircase—all hurled into one busy-bodied bundle—and head off to wherever their final landing place is. All before I even set one foot off the train and onto the gum-stained platform.

I too jog up the stairs, only not as swiftly as the bundle of people before me. Once at the top, I cross the busy intersection, making my way into Central Park. It's been a few months since I participated in park yoga and was lucky to be able to book my spot online this morning. I can feel my zen completely off its game—my soul craves a yogafying boost, much like a vampire craves blood. Especially after Sebastian bitch-slapped me with the news he signed me up to work with Jonathan Knight.

Central Park Yoga is growing increasingly popular. There is nothing better than hanging out with a group of zen-minded individuals, basking in the commonality of our love of yoga and love of the serene oasis that is Central Park. Two years ago, Yoga in the Park was free, but now it has become this sort of exclusive event where you have to purchase tickets ahead of time or pay for a spot on the grass online. Some organize special yoga in the park parties where afterwards you hang out and eat a fancy organic picnic lunch. I've never had time to attend one of the parties, but perhaps I will now, and post a review about the organic picnic lunch.

I find my way to the group, right in front of Morse statue. There are at least forty other yogis here, of all ages, ready to breathe and stretch themselves into metaphysical nirvana. I hand the instructor the ticket I purchased online and claim a spot between a young girl and an older man. I unroll my pink-and-white yoga-mat and begin my zen rejuvenation.

An hour and thirty minutes later, I stand in *BookBender*, a trendy Manhattan bookstore, across the way from Central Park, sipping a spinach, banana, and pomegranate smoothie. Yoga left me feeling incredibly renewed and redefined, as though I had some sort of a psychedelic mental-orgasm. Whatever the case, it has sprung forth a good measure of comprehensibility.

I now believe I *can* pull this off—be an effectual restaurant consultant to Jonathan Knight, offering invaluable insight to him and his restaurant…just as soon as I find this book that, according to what I researched on Google, should help. Oh yes—here it is.

Restaurant Consulting for Dummies.

Yep. That oughta do it.

CHAPTER 7

"I can't believe you actually spent twenty-five bucks on this book," Sebastian says, arbitrarily perusing the pages of *Restaurant Consulting for Dummies.*

The two of us are having lunch at a trendy diner downstairs from Manifique. He FaceTime'd me as I was leaving BookBender to see if I was available for, "a working lunch to review and strategize my role with the Firm," is how he prefaced it. I agreed since yoga successfully steamrolled my temporary aversion toward him.

Although, at this moment, I'm glaring at Sebastian, feeling a tad perplexed. I mean why is it *so* hard to believe I paid for the book? Honestly, I need it. Surely any right-minded individual understands my dilemma. It's not like I can put on a hat that says "restaurant consultant" and—*poof*—I'm instantly a restaurant consultant. If that's the case, I'd ecstatically put on a hat that says Doctor, Lawyer, Carrie Bradshaw (strolling along the busy sidewalks of Manhattan with that fashion-savvy confidence), Adele (love her), a Food Network Contest Judge (not any one in particular), Beyoncé (love her too), or even a freaking dog groomer. Okay, might as well scratch dog groomer—but only because I'm highly allergic to most dogs.

"Well, don't get your boxer briefs in a bundle, Sir Sebastian. I didn't actually spend twenty-five bucks on it." I matter-of-factly proclaim, before piggishly taking a bite out of the tuna on rye sandwich the cute girl behind the front counter recommended. "Book-Bender was having a massive sale today. I paid only eleven dollars and sixty-five cents on it." I reach into my BookBender bag, boastfully revealing three more items I purchased. "I even got this lovely journal and pen, and this resourceful cookbook called *Take Out Food at Home*. It has a chicken marsala recipe I think you'll appreciate."

"Well, *muchas gracias*, babe—plumb sweet of you." He takes a sip of his Shirley Temple and winks at me. "It's so ladylike of you to pick me up a little somethin' somethin', even when you probably felt like throwing crap in my face."

He's right. I actually *did* imagine throwing crap in his face. It just so happened to be my visual mantra during yoga.

"Yeah. But I'm totally over the whole Jonathan thing now. Which is why I got the book. I'm adapting to my new title. *Restaurant Consultant*." The two words roll off my tongue as though they are some kooky adaptation of a foreign language.

Sebastian smiles wryly, takes a final bite of his kale and apple salad, then reaches into his spiffy Boconi messenger bag, unearthing a large white envelope labeled *Kennedy Prescott*. He covertly slides it over to me, as if the envelope holds information meant only to be seen by highly classified eyes.

Maybe it does.

Sebastian raises his eyebrows and gestures his head in a motion that seems to suggest, "Go ahead now. Open it."

"So, can't I finish my lunch first?"

"Working lunch," he adamantly reclaims. "Just open it up and take a look," he adds, catching a quick glance at his watch.

I sneak in the last bite of my dill pickle, wipe my hands and mouth with a napkin, and animatedly tear into the mystery envelope.

And right after I pull out a small stack of papers, held together by a dark blue star-shaped paper clip, I glance up at Sebastian questioningly.

"What's all of this?"

He leans back into the booth cushion, carefully nursing the rest of his Shirley Temple. "It's your employment package."

Curiously, I remove the paper clip and review the stack of papers that consist of the following:

1. A detailed report on Jonathan Knight's business goals
2. A Confidentiality Agreement
3. A Compensation Agreement for Independent Contractors
4. A printout containing a Restaurant Consultant job description
5. Manifique's Code of Conduct and Ethics
6. A list of Manifique employees
7. Four pages torn out of *Vogue London* featuring young women adorned in fancy businesslike attire

"You can review and sign the Agreements and Code of Conduct and Ethics and just give them to me anytime before next week when you officially start," Sebastian says, bringing my attention from the stack of papers and back to him.

"Right. And what day is that exactly...when I officially start?"

Sebastian takes a deep breath, closes his eyes, and delicately mumbles under his breath, "Monday morning."

I raise my eyebrows and widen my eyes, showcasing my astonishment, then swallow the lump of shock that's positioned itself in the center of my throat. "So soon? Wow, I'd thought I would have at least a few weeks to fully prepare."

Or perhaps try to perfect my restaurant-consulting skills on someone else—someone who is not Jonathan Knight. Reasonable thought, right?

"You have the rest of this week and the weekend to research and prepare. You've got this, Penelope," Sebastian says, sounding quite convincing.

He reaches back into his messenger bag, adding, "Ooh, I can't believe I almost forgot to give you this, as well." His blue eyes glisten, flamboyantly exemplifying his amusement.

He tosses over another envelope, much smaller than the mystery one. It contains a corporate credit card, a wad of cash, and a cute little Manifique employee badge that says Kennedy Prescott—Restaurant Consultant.

Playfully, I attach the name badge to my T-shirt, but mentally question the wad of cash and the corporate credit card. I suppose my facial expression provides Sebastian a clue of my uncertainty because he explains soon after, "I know you're wondering about the bundle of dough and the credit card."

I offer a gentle nod in agreement.

"Okay, girlfriend, we've gotta work fast to get you all primed and prodded for your assignment." He rubs his hands together, gearing up for some big-time revelation. "That being said, you've got a couple of pre-assignments to complete prior to Monday."

"Primed and Prodded? That sounds like a kinky book title. You know, like a follow-up series to Fifty Shades, perhaps?" I say, mocking Sebastian's seriousness.

"Penelope, I'm being totally for real now—concentrate, woman! First, the corporate credit card. Some time before Monday, go back to Diamonattos. Tonya is eagerly awaiting your arrival. Use the four pages from *Vogue* for inspiration and she will help you get some new business-consultant-like outfits. Use the corporate credit card for that."

"Okay. Sounds easy enough. What about the wad of cash?"

"Right. That. So, I need you to go to Jonathan's restaurant."

"Wait. What? When? I assumed I was to meet with him Monday."

"Yes, well you *are* to meet with him then."

I beam a contentious gaze at Sebastian, striking him like lightning.

He shifts uncomfortably in his seat, "B-but," he stammers apprehensively at first, "given your history with Jonathan—well with the restaurant specifically—I strongly suggest your Monday morning meeting is from a fresh perspective. A clean slate, so to speak."

"A clean slate?" I pause for an instant, pensively evaluating his advisement.

The last time I was in Jonathan Knight's "esteemed" restaurant was just over a year ago.

And it was crap.

All of it.

The food, the decor, the staff—the entire experience. I walked—no,

I fled his restaurant with a horrible impression. One I won't soon forget.

So perhaps Sebastian makes a good case. A clean slate is in order. A tall order.

"Okay, you're right, especially if I am going to be of service to him."

"Oh wonderful! So you'll go now?"

"Now? As in right this moment? I-I can't go *now*," I protest.

"Sure, you can. Going now in *that* outfit, is perfect. You totally look like some normal girl, out for a bite to eat."

Just then I realize I'm still dressed in my yoga-in-the-park gear: yoga pants, a long T-shirt, Sketchers, sunglasses, and an *I Love New York* baseball cap.

"Right again," I mumble. "But I just pigged out on lunch," I mention, clearly looking for another way out.

"Penelope, you know how this shit works. You go and freaking assess the situation. Service, and whatever else it is *you people* look at. You don't have to just eat."

I giggle internally and move past his "you people" remark. Yet, once again, Sebastian makes a good point. I'll go to specifically appraise the restaurant's service, decor, menu, food—to evaluate the experience as it is now and attempt to remove the pitiful recollection of my last visit—now etched in my memory like a bad tattoo.

Sebastian looks at his watch and eases out of the booth. "Look, I'm gonna be late for my afternoon meeting. Are we good here? Will you go today? I mean, I truly think you should. Use the cash to pay for your transportation and for the meal. I highly suggest you Uber."

"Alright. And yes, it's all good. I'll go now." I slide out of the booth, gather my belongings, and walk out of the diner with Sebastian.

"Great, doll face. Update me tonight back at home?"

"Of course."

Sebastian gives me a hug then runs toward the elevators, making his way back up to Manifique's headquarters.

The sticky humid air New York is known for in July hits me like a freight train as I exit the building and climb into the Uber car.

Why did you agree to do this? You're a Food Critic not a Restaurant

Consultant, my spunky conscience taunts, while my more sensible conscience argues, *Don't worry, your minor in Food Studies, your keen business sense, and innate passion for food have more than prepared you for this.*

For the entire twenty-six minute drive into TriBeCa, I blindly stare out the window, lost in my own sequence of thoughts. Which side of my conscience is right? Spunk or Sensibility?

"Um…Miss?" The Uber Driver's voice breaks up the pungent scrimmage in my head. "We've arrived. Your destination—Knight and Daze Grill and Bar."

CHAPTER 8

J enter Jonathan Knight's restaurant—Knight and Daze Grill and Bar—with exuberant confidence. As if the world is mine and mine alone.

Okay. Not really.

In fact, I'm still on the sidewalk, near the entrance—right where the Uber driver dropped me off only moments ago. Since then, I've been pacing the industrial concrete, back and forth with my phone glued to my ear, pretending to be engrossed in an important phone conversation, as unsuspecting passers-by maneuver their way around me.

I can't seem to bring myself to open the doors and walk in.

I know—I'm utterly hopeless.

Well maybe hopeless is a bit melodramatic—even for me. Truth is, my nerves are shattered, as though someone reached inside of me, grabbed all of my nerves, and dumped them onto the ground, breaking them into minuscule fragments that will undoubtedly take ages to restore.

Yet, in an effort to keep from appearing like a crazy woman to all of TriBeCa, I decide to plop down onto one of the park-like benches outside of the restaurant's main entrance. Ironically, the last time I was here, I sat on this exact bench as I waited for the restaurant pager to vibrate when my table was ready. It was a one-hour wait back then, despite my reservation. And sitting here now brings forth a vivid reflection of that evening.

I had previously dined at just about all of the restaurants in TriBeCa and was fervently prepared to dine at Knight and Daze, one of NY's finest eateries. The streets of TriBeCa were livelier than ever —a warm Spring night in April—the last weekend of the TriBeCa Film Festival. The Festival seemed to call attention to an already trendy part of Manhattan. A pleasant mix of creatives visiting from out of town, celebrities, and residents colorfully garnished the streets, shops, and restaurants.

Observing their cheerful faces put a smile on my own, even though I was feeling especially down. Garrett was to join me that evening—well actually, he was to join me for the entire weekend. We had booked a night's stay at the Sheraton, a festival film screening the next day, and to jumpstart the weekend, we reserved a table here. Our dinner reservation was to be all pleasure—no business. Writing a review was not at all part of the plan. But Garrett cancelled at the last minute, claiming he encountered some sort of an emergency. *Had the scumbag been cheating on me back then?*

Even though Garrett cancelled, I decided a weekend getaway to TriBeCa was something I didn't want to pass up. Once I arrived that Saturday, I was famished and was looking forward to a fabulous meal and experience at Knight and Daze; to my disappointment, it was far from what I expected.

I shake the flashback loose from my head, reminding myself I'm here now to forget all of that—to embark on a journey that will produce a much different, clean-slate perspective.

Hopefully.

My iPhone's distinctive ringtone jolts me back into a state of reality. And of course it's Sebastian beckoning via FaceTime.

"Yes?" I say as his jolly face appears on the screen of my phone.

Sebastian seems to be surveying my surroundings. "Yep. I had a feeling your ass was stalling. Get in there, woman! Go assess the hell out of that place."

He knows me all too well. A perk, and at times, a disadvantage of having a perfectly astute BFF.

"I will, Sebastian."

"What's the holdup anyway?"

I pause to think of a reasonable excuse for my hopelessness. "Nothing really. I'm just enjoying TriBeCa."

"Mmm-hmm. I thought you could use some encouragement. So, go on. Get in there. Like now. Okay?"

I nod, even though I'm not in total agreement.

"Alright then, sexy. I'll catch ya later." He blows me a kiss before magically ending his FaceTime intervention.

After taking in a few calming deep breaths, I finally walk into Knight and Daze.

"Are you meeting someone here, or will you be eating alone today?" says the not-so-friendly young girl as I approach the hostess station in the restaurant lobby. She appears to be about sixteen or seventeen with pink streaks in her already platinum-blond hair, a prominent studded diamond attached to her nose, and an attitude that screams rebel. She offers no smile and seems to be annoyed by my existence. As if I'm an interruption to her life.

"No, I'll be dining alone today."

She shrugs her shoulders and hands me a menu. "Alrighty then. Follow me. I'll seat you."

As directed, I trail behind her rudeness through the lobby and into the restaurant's main seating area. The entire place looks dark, cold, and old, mimicking something a tad medieval.

She seats me in a corner booth, in front of a large bay window, bypassing at least two-dozen empty tables. It appears I'm their only customer—a red flag observation that concerns me. *Why aren't they busy?*

"So, I'm Olivia. I'll be your server today." She flings her overgrown bangs off her face. "You want some water?" she asks, her mouth full of chewing gum.

"Um, sure. And coffee. May I have coffee too, please?"

"Yeah, but that may take a few minutes. No one really orders coffee this time of the day so I'll have to ask them to brew a fresh pot," she says before walking away from my table toward what I assume is the kitchen.

I send a quick text to Sebastian.

Me: Okay. I'm inside and it's not off to a dynamite start.

Moments later he replies.

Sebastian: Brilliant. May you find pleasure in helping him get his shit together. xo

Seconds later, Miss Rude Girl returns with a glass of water. "You know what you want yet?" she says, her eyes glued to activity outside of the booth's window. There are at least five other restaurants across the street—all quite busy with patrons dining on exquisite-looking patio tables. As she peers out the window, her eyes light up as a child's does when they see snow for the first time.

"Not quite. I'm still deciding. What do you recommend?"

"Um, me? Oh well, I really haven't had much to eat here lately. But I hear the pan-seared salmon is good. And it's part of the lunch menu available until 4."

"What else comes with the pan-seared salmon?" I ask, trying hard to get past her lack of great customer service skills.

"Baked potato and vegetables," she says after popping a large bubble of gum. "Oh and a small side salad," she adds as if it's an afterthought.

"Okay then, I'll have that. Butter and chives on the side, please."

"No problem. I'll have them start that now. I'll be back with your coffee too. Oh and I hope milk is okay. We are apparently out of cream. Again." She takes my menu and marches toward the kitchen.

After Olivia returns with my coffee and walks back toward the hostess station, I remove the brand new journal and pen from my BookBender bag and begin taking notes.

KNIGHT AND DAZE GRILL and Bar

Service: abrupt

Decor: stuffy

Menu: insipid

Overall appeal: not a damn thing

As I NOTE my introductory assessment, thoughts veer back to my last visit here. *Has nothing even changed?*

After about twenty minutes, Olivia delivers my food. "So, here's your food. If you need something else just holler."

"Thanks Olivia," I say as she walks toward the hostess station.

I stare at the plate of food in utter disbelief. It does nothing to suggest this is something one would expect from a restaurant once deemed five-star. And besides being barely lukewarm, the pan-seared salmon is bland and genuinely unappealing. How can one advertise pan-seared when it's missing the actual *sear*? The baked potato is probably the best item on the plate as the vegetables are mushy and frail looking. And the salad? Overly wilted and brown. I don't even attempt to drink the coffee—I don't like coffee with milk.

Ugh.

No wonder this place is empty. I mean, who would want to eat here? Anyone would be better off eating a TV dinner at home.

I place my napkin on top of the plate, pushing it to the edge of the table, hoping to get Olivia's attention.

She approaches, "Done already?"

"Yes. I suppose I'm not as hungry as I thought I was," I say convincingly.

"Oh. Okay then would you like to take it to-go?" she asks, seeming to be genuinely concerned.

"Um, no thank you. I'll just take the check now."

Olivia nods, takes the plate into the kitchen, and returns a few minutes later with my check. "I forgot to ask you if you'd like some dessert."

"Oh no. I couldn't. But thanks anyway."

She smiles and places the check on the edge of the table.

"Olivia, can I ask you a question?"

"Sure, I guess."

"Does it get busy here? Like the restaurants across the street?"

"Us? Busy?" She holds her hand over her mouth as though she's trying hard to stifle a giggle. "Uh, no. Not for a while now. You're the only customer we've had all day."

"Oh I see. Well, thank you." I smile and pay, using the cash Sebastian provided earlier.

By the time I arrive back home, I am welcomed by the tantalizing scent of bacon and find Sebastian in the kitchen cooking.

"Hey, sunshine. Care for some bacon and eggs? I had this unrelenting craving for breakfast. I'm making my bad-ass bacon, mushroom, spinach, and cheese omelette."

"Breakfast for dinner? Sounds perfect."

"I take it you didn't eat much at Knight and Daze?" he asks, cracking eggs into a glass mixing bowl. He's wearing a blue and white *Move over Martha Stewart* apron I got him for Christmas a few years ago. Sebastian loves to cook and the bacon, mushroom, spinach, and cheese omelette just so happens to be his specialty.

"No. The food was entirely inedible. Cold and bland," I explain, grabbing a bottle of water out of the fridge.

"Ooooh. Gross. No wonder Jonathan's come to Manifique for help."

"Right. And the hostess was incredibly rude. I felt like I was a mere interruption to her day."

Sebastian shakes his head in disbelief as he cuts up spinach into bite-size pieces.

"Seems like nothing has changed. In fact, I get the impression things have worsened since my last visit."

"What was your experience like last time? Do you still have that review?" He cuts up mushrooms and the bacon into bite-size pieces.

"Yes, its in a file on my iPad. Want me to read it to you?"

"If you don't mind," he says as he artfully prepares our omelettes.

I retrieve my iPad from the living-room coffee table, nestle onto the barstool, take a long sip of water, and gear up to read Sebastian the review I gave Knight and Daze Grill and Bar last April.

"You ready?"

"Yep. Go for it, " he says as he places our delectable-looking plates of omelettes onto the counter and parks himself on the barstool next to me.

I take a bite of the omelette and begin reading Sebastian the review.

KNIGHT AND DAZE GRILL AND BAR - *My Less Than-To-Be Desired Encounter.*

A weekend set aside to partake in TriBeCa Film Festival activities was to be kicked off with an elegant meal at the well-esteemed, five-star glory, known to locals as Knight and Daze.

Admittedly, I didn't set forth on this venture donning my 'food critic' hat. It was just me—Penelope Monroe—the TriBeCa tourist. However, I would not be doing a service by letting anyone walk into this dive-in-disguise without being candidly forewarned.

Of all of the words I can use to summarize Knight and Daze, there is only one word that sticks. P-O-O-R.

P - as in Punk'd. I could not help thinking Ashton Kutcher was lurking somewhere behind the scenes with a film crew recording a debut remake of Punk'd. Surely that had to be the only reasonable explanation for the unbelievable candid-camera-like experience.

O - as in beyond Overrated. I mean I was expecting gold on a plate. But instead, was served seaweed over a bed of bitter sticky-ness. Oh wait, was that supposed to be a Black Pepper Crusted Ahi Tuna Steak over a bed of Shrimp Risotto? Total Epic Fail.

O - as in Outrageously overpriced. I reluctantly paid fifty-five bucks on the mishmash they called elegant cuisine—after I strongly considered performing a juvenile dine and dash. Although, if I did that and got caught, my jailhouse meal would have been better received. Probably.

R - as in the ultimate Repugnance. Need I say more?

The two-hour experience left me feeling jilted. Like a beautiful bride left hanging at the altar. But go if you must. That is if you feel the need to witness where not to eat. To be honest, I'm not sure how Knight and Daze Grill and Bar came to receive its merited rating. It's far from five stars. Perhaps a one star? But only by default—it is located in pristine TriBeCa, after all.

If by reading this, I have saved you from this travesty—you're welcome. Glad I can be of service.

Until next time—Cheers to you and yours!

There is a short pause as Sebastian finishes off the last bite of his omelette.

He looks at me wide-eyed and says, "Hot damn, woman. No wonder he fucking hates you."

THE FIFTY-TWO WEEK Chronicles - FaceBook Page

July 25, 2016

A mind-cleansing stroll down the streets of Manhattan last week led me to Restaurant Row and into a tiny treasure known as FlashBurger.

Don't let the name fool you. It's not your average burger joint. In fact there is nothing average about this cream of the burger crop. Flash-Burger is world-class—Burger Therapy—a new edition to the 'For The Soul' series. Yep that's right—Burgers and Fries For The Soul.

And respectable organically-savvy therapy is their licensed area of expertise. I mean everything on the menu is organic and oh so natural. Even the beverages.

There's only one word needed to rightfully summarize my lunch: Mmmmmmm-licious.

So go today, if you can. Or tomorrow. Or whenever you're in need of something therapeutic—or thera-FOOD-ic?

The eats, staff, and ambiance, of FlashBurger is a five-star remedy.

Cheers to you and yours!

Part Two

"Life gives you lots of chances to screw up, which means you have just as many chances to get it right."
    Carrie Bradshaw - Sex and the City

CHAPTER 9

"*I* fucking *hate* her."

Those are the first four words that shoot out of Jonathan Knight's mouth, like a loose cannon, upon our initial introduction.

At least I can only *assume* he's Jonathan Knight by the brazen inscription of the letters J-O-N-A-T-H-A-N sewn onto the top upper left corner of the white chef coat he is befittingly sporting. We haven't quite made it to the *actual* introduction. You know, the less impromptu one I rehearsed at least one-hundred and thirty-six thousand times over the past few days, including on the subway ride to TriBeCa this morning.

The one that should have included me walking into the back office of Knight and Daze, coming face to face with Jonathan, my hand extended for a firm, restaurant consultant-like handshake.

The one in which I ingeniously prepared myself to say, "Hello, I'm Kennedy Prescott (my fake, clever under-disguise name), it's a pleasure to meet you. I look forward to working with you on reaching your restaurant image improvement goals."

The one I wholeheartedly imagined would have started off *nothing* at all like this.

Nor did I conceptualize Jonathan to be the handsomely hunky type with wavy, dark hair, entrancing blue eyes, perfectly shaped lips, and just enough facial hair to be alluringly pleasing to my eyes.

No, when I devised this extremely unpredictable moment, I mentally casted Jonathan's cameo role to be played by an old and stuffy brute with oily hair, a scruffy beard, a few missing teeth, and a protruding beer belly. Not Mr. Tall, Dark, and Delicious.

"I'm sorry? You hate her? Um, who?" I finally manage to render, underarms sweating through my white oxford button-down shirt. *Thank God for Degree antiperspirant.*

I nervously adjust the black oval-framed eyeglasses Sebastian commissioned me to wear, citing "they add a spark of smarts to my appearance".

Spark of Smarts? Makes me instantly think back to *Bring It On* and those ridiculously flamboyant *Jazz Hands.*

Jonathan looks up briefly from his desk chair, as he nonchalantly leans back, his legs resting comfortably across the top half of the small oak desk as his eyes hold a hawk-like gaze to the iPad he's holding. He looks at me again—a double take—and quickly shifts his legs and feet to the stained concrete floor, fumbles his iPad onto the desk, and rises from the now noticeably squeaky chair to a respectable stance.

I suppose he didn't fully realize I stepped into his office.

"Um, excuse me." He clears his throat. Immediately, I can't help but notice his voice has a sexy edge to it with a delectable bite of New York sassiness. "Who are you?"

"Hello. I'm Kennedy Prescott." I step over to his desk, extend my hand out for a firm restaurant-consultant-like handshake. "It's a pleasure to meet you. I look forward to working with you on reaching your restaurant image improvement goals."

I mentally pat myself on the back, especially pleased those words came out as rehearsed. Despite the fact my voice probably mimicked an assiduous robot. Practice *kind of* makes perfect.

He slips his hand from my handshaking death-grip, moves from behind his desk, and approaches me.

As he invades my personal space, my senses can't help but capture the captivating smell of body wash, cologne, and...cilantro, perhaps?

"Hi there." He chuckles slightly. "I'm Jonathan Knight and I too am pleased to meet you... Kennedy, you said?"

I nervously bop my head yes and fold my arms, not quite sure what to do with them. "Um yes, Prescott. Kennedy Prescott."

"Cool name, " he says and produces a half smile, as though he's imagining something sinister.

I swallow the miniature lump in my throat and ask, "So, who is this *her* you hate?"

He shakes his head as if he's trying to wake up from an illicit daydream. "Oh that. Just pay it no mind. I was only thinking out loud. I had no idea you were here actually." He walks back over to his desk and grabs his iPad. "How did you get in here anyway?"

"A gentleman was leaving out of the back door. A vendor, I assume? I just walked right in. I'm sorry about that...I um...I didn't mean to intrude." I say, feeling as though I've been a bad student who has been sent to the principal's office.

Jonathan sits down on his desk chair and looks at me questionably. "That was Manny, my produce vendor. And you're here early. I wasn't quite expecting you for at least another twenty minutes. But no worries. I'm really glad you're here."

I smile, acknowledging his statement. Then I steal a moment to take in my surroundings. In all the years I have spent obsessing over food, never have I stepped foot in the back of the house. The behind-the-scenes or central command center in a restaurant. It's like the backstage area of a Broadway play. And right now, I have a VIP pass. I try hard to conceal my excitement by maintaining a cool and collected pokerface—which, by the way, I also rehearsed.

"Penelope Monroe," Jonathan says, jerking me out of my back-of-the-house groupie mind-trip.

And did he just say Penelope Monroe? As in *me*?

Wait. Does he know who I *really* am?

Shit. Shit. Shit. Okay, wait a minute. Whatever you do, don't panic. No need to stop, drop, and roll up on out of here...yet.

"I'm sorry?" I say, taking a chance I heard him incorrectly.

"Penelope Monroe. She's the *her* I hate. I was talking about Penelope Monroe when you walked in."

I stand here facing him in utter disbelief. I mean I only suspected he hated me, but hearing him say it—

"You do know who she is, right?"

Awkward.

"Um yes, I've heard of her." I mumble, feeling the blood rush to my cheeks.

"Here. Look at this." He abruptly stands, still holding his iPad, walks over to where I'm standing and emphatically shows me my own Fifty-Two Week Chronicles Facebook Page. "She posted this today. FlashBurger? Can you believe it? How can FlashBurger get a five-star rating and I get—"

He stops talking, takes a deep breath, runs his fingers through his sexy hair, and tosses his iPad back onto the desk.

"You uh, follow her Facebook page?" I ask in an effort to stifle the mood.

"Yep. We all do. Chefs, I mean. We all follow her and that Gregory Hambrick guy. Anyway, you know what I really want from you?"

"What?" I ask, feeling as though I'll do anything he wants as long as he stops talking about the *real* me to the fake me.

"I want you to help get my restaurant a mention on her new page. Word is, since she no longer works for *The Bee*, she'll only post a good review each week via that Page. Mine needs to be one of the restaurants Penelope Monroe reviews. Can you help me achieve that?" The look in his eyes is obstinate and, for a brief moment, they take me on a high speed ride into his soul.

I pause to digest his request and think back to the review I gave the restaurant last year. My mere words—an opinionated assessment —have altered his life. And all Jonathan can fathom is the opportunity to have me—Penelope Monroe—publicly acclaim his restaurant.

"Yes. Of course," I say, feeling as though I've been injected with a potent dose of mind-altering reality. "However, it's going to take a great deal of effort on your part. You may not like some of the things I suggest and at times you'll have to—" I clear my throat and adjust the stupid *spark of smarts* eyeglasses. "Well, you'll simply have to swallow your pride."

Jonathan approaches, invading my personal space once again, and extends his hand for a handshake. "You've got a deal, Ms. Kennedy Prescott. And by the way, " his voice lowers to an almost whisper while his perfectly shaped lips curve into a mischievous smirk, " I like your glasses. They make you look playful, mysterious, and smart."

CHAPTER 10

"You smell a bit like cilantro," I say, embarrassed I allowed those words to charge out of my mouth like a runaway locomotive.

"Oh. Well yeah, Manny delivered fresh cilantro," Jonathan replies, evidently unfazed by my cheeky outburst. "We use it for our signature salsa as well as for a few other dishes. Would you like to taste some?"

"Cilantro? Um, no thanks."

Jonathan laughs, and I can't help but catch a glimpse of his perfectly white teeth. *God, he's absolutely dreamy.*

"No, I mean the salsa. Would you like to taste some of our Wicked Salsa? It's a brand new recipe."

Of course he meant the salsa, you big dummy. Stop focusing on his looks and focus on restaurant stuff...you imposter.

"Oh right. Salsa. Sure, I'll try some," I say, feeling a little out of my element.

Jonathan leads the way out of his office and into the sizable kitchen area where he disappears into a spacious walk-in cooler.

He reappears seconds later, toting a bulky rectangular container that he places alongside a small bowl of tortilla chips resting on top of the stainless steel prep counter.

Curiosity guides me over to the prep table where he snags a chip, dunks it into the Wicked Salsa and commands an authoritative "open wide," before shoving the fire-laced chip into my mouth.

At first, it tastes like your average chip and salsa. Then, without warning, my taste buds are propelled into a flavor-town utopia. The Wicked Salsa has the ideal balance of tomatoes, jalapeño peppers, onions, salt, garlic, cilantro, lime juice, and something else my palate can't quite identify. I close my eyes, only momentarily, entranced by the rave-like party happening in my mouth.

Jonathan smiles, looking thoroughly gratified by my expression. "What do you think?"

"Honestly? It's sinfully good," I admit, extremely timid to ask for more than what was placed in my mouth.

A recollection of my last two dining experiences here rattles my unrelenting thirst for knowledge. I mean why did those visits go so drastically awry?

"Jonathan, is there somewhere we can chat? I'd really like to strategize some of your short-term and long-term goals."

Jonathan covers the container of Wicked Salsa and winks at me. "Of course. The restaurant doesn't open for another couple of hours. We can talk up in the front." He carries the salsa container to the walk-in cooler and opens the huge industrial door. "Just pick a table. I'll join you in a second... After I brew us some fresh coffee."

"Coffee?" *I hope you have cream today*, I think to myself, pleased I didn't blurt that out in the same fashion as I did the cilantro remark.

"Yeah, coffee. You do drink coffee, right?"

I nod yes. "With cream and two sugars please."

"Coming right up."

Moments later, Jonathan accompanies me at a booth next to a window in the dining room area. He places two white mugs inscribed Knight and Daze, a pint-sized carafe of cream, a couple of spoons, two packets of sugar, and a coffee press filled with coffee onto the table before he smoothly glides into the booth.

"I must confess, a spiffy coffee press is the last device I'd expect to find in your kitchen gadget arsenal."

Jonathan peers up at me, briefly, as he concentrates on pouring us both coffee, his eyes revealing playful discontent. "I learned to appreciate the art of brewing the perfect cup of coffee while I studied Culinary Arts in Paris several years ago." He smiles wryly with glaring eyes, as if he knows his comment would throw me in a mental spin.

Somehow his revelation makes me feel as though I fell short on the research side of things.

I should have used Google. Duh.

"Paris?" I say as he slides a mug over to me; the coffee's pleasant aroma immediately commands my senses—*drink me*. I give in and bask in the rich flavor.

"Yep. Paris. I studied at *Le Cordon Bleu* right after high school. I knew at a young age I loved cooking as an art. It was a passion of mine."

"Was?"

"You're highly perceptive, Ms. Prescott. And yes, it *was* a passion of mine. It still is—most days anyway." He shrugs his shoulders, wraps his strong hands tightly around the mug, and looks down, deep in thought. "But not as much as I'd like it to be."

"So...what's changed?" I cautiously probe with high hopes of unlocking the reason why Knight and Daze has seemingly dwindled, like a once-blooming flower allowed to simply wither away.

Jonathan takes a sip of his coffee, "A lot has changed. More than I care to discuss right at the moment. Rain check? I'd much rather discuss my short-term and long-term goals...per your suggestion."

Insert record scratch...

I try to study his expression but, at this moment his eyes appear cold, revealing nothing credible. "Right. Goals. Okay, so shall we begin with your short-term goals?" I ask, veering to full-on Restaurant Consultant mode.

"Short-term is simple. Improve my image and my restaurant's image. Long-term, also pretty simple. Maintain said newly improved image." He then produces that sexy smirk I'm growing fond of. "How's your coffee?"

"Oh yes, well it's quite scrumptious actually. The press certainly makes a huge difference. Plus I detect something unique—cinnamon perhaps?"

He raises both brows and nods, "Yes, you've got a noticeable palate. Cinnamon, a touch of nutmeg, and a hint of dark chocolate. It's our signature blend. *Java Man Joe.*"

Java Man Joe was not the coffee Olivia served me—well at least I don't think so because I never tasted it. And *Wicked Salsa*? I don't recall these items called out anywhere on the Knight and Daze menu. *Why?*

"Jonathan, I believe the best way for me to help you achieve your short-term, long-term, and any other goals you may have not yet realized, is that I become fully engulfed in your business."

"Fully engulfed... How?" He asks, appearing to be slightly uncomfortable with my claim. Still, according to *Restaurant Consulting For Dummies*, in order for me to be resultant in my approach in aiding in the restaurant's restoration, I must consummately soak up all aspects of the business - soup to nuts. I need to become one with the establishment.

"Well, simply put, I need to become part of your team," I reveal, "—just for a couple of days, until I have a thorough grasp on how operations are...as it stands today."

Looking at Jonathan's whole face light up, seeming to be amused by my spiel, almost frightens me. Once again, what the hell am I thinking? I know nothing about actually *working* in a restaurant. And somehow I'm convinced Jonathan is more than aware of this not-so-minor technicality.

"Fair enough," Jonathan offers, a cynical tone to his hardy voice. His arms are folded, and his brows embossed conspiratorially. "Shall we begin in the kitchen?"

CHAPTER 11

"*S*hit just got kinda real...little lady," Sebastian's words dispatch through the speaker of my iPhone like an all-points bulletin. And the term *real* is an absolute understatement.

You see, I decided to call on Sebastian a few minutes ago to talk me down from the ledge of *freaking-out-now* that I am most certainly about to dive off of.

"Yeah, I know!" I practically whisper into my iPhone as I scrutinize my reflection in the mirror inside of the ladies' restroom. I'm changing into a white chef coat Jonathan provided me a few minutes ago. You know, like right after I foolishly declared I need to be thrown into all parts of the business like fresh meat tossed to a pack of hungry wolves. Besides all of that, the chef coat is about two sizes too large. I look like I'm all draped up to partake in some type of culinary science experiment...on planet Uranus.

Sebastian snickers, sounding annoyingly entertained. "And explain again how you got yourself into this fascinating quandary?"

"I'm really glad you find this humorous." I buck in sarcasm, rolling my eyes in disgust. As I lean against the bathroom wall, I notice a small window above one of the stalls. "Meanwhile I'm over here, laying out my escape plan. I can easily fit through the window, you know. Need I remind you it's a *Monday*? For crying out loud, I really should be at home, curled up under the covers where it's safe."

"Sweetie, please snap a selfie and send it to me," Sebastian interjects, blatantly ignoring my academy-award-worthy rant. "I'm dying to see you in that chef coat. It's been a tough morning and a good gut-busting laugh is what the doctor ordered. That along with another green tea latte."

"Sebastian really, I need your vote of confidence," I plead, dodging the austere request flung my way. "I know in order to help Jonathan, being enthralled into all parts of his business is essential." I slowly ease my back down the wall and sit on the cold tile floor. "But at the moment I'm feeling overwhelmed."

"I'm sorry, baby girl. You've got this. And trust me, if I didn't think you, of all people, could help him, you wouldn't be there today. So tell me your plan."

My plan. I bite my nails.

"Right. My plan." I stand and begin to nervously pace the tile floor as I quickly devise a course of action. "Well, I suppose I'll spend most of today observing and learning all about the kitchen, the chefs, the recipes, and the roles of Jonathan's employees."

"Then go get 'em, doll. Break a sexy leg."

I end my call with Sebastian, but somehow feel our conversation was far more therapeutic for him than it was for me. I take a final once-over in the mirror, maneuver my long hair into a crafty bun, adjust the eye-glasses that keep slipping down the bridge of my nose, and say to my reflection, "You, my lady, have got this shit."

The next few hours seem to speedily pass by, like one of those high-tech, fast-motion video clips I sometimes watch on YouTube. I've shadowed almost everyone on every back-of-the-house station so far, which has garnered a respectable appreciation for the harsh demands restaurant work encompasses. As a food critic, I am categorically influenced by a restaurant's service, atmosphere, value, and the fundamental execution of food advertised on the menu. However today, I've ceremonially gathered it's so much more than all of that.

* * *

By 4PM, I feel physically debilitated, as if I'd finally participated in the New York City Marathon. My hair is emphatically awry, and both sides of what was once the white oversized chef coat are now artfully splattered with an array of colors—the aftermath of having unsightly collisions with all but one of the servers. I'm pretty sure I look like a walking abstract painting.

Jonathan encourages me to sit for a break and, after several of his failed attempts, I finally agree without further protest.

I remove the chef coat and stuff it into my bag, hoping I find some energy to wash it at home tonight. And after finding a booth in the back of the restaurant, I plunge into it like I'm its oreo cookie and it's my cold glass of milk.

With my aching back sinking into the comfort of the booth's cushion, I lie here, eyes shut, melting in the amenity of quiet relaxation—today's rare commodity that is mine for the taking.

Jonathan's hunky voice interrupts my moment of quietude. "Would you like some refreshments? I come bearing coffee and tiramisu cheesecake bites."

At once, I pop up, feeling instantly revived. I mean even the walking dead probably can't resist cheesecake.

He places two mugs of coffee and a plate with two petite portions of cheesecake, capped with a dollop of cocoa dusted whipped cream, onto the center of the table. My mouth waters at the sight and smell each item conjures.

"I added cream and two packets of sugar to your coffee. That is how you take yours, right?"

I nod yes, as I grab hold of the mug he slides over to me and offer a smile in appreciation.

He sits down across from me with a skeptical look to his expressive eyes. "You look exhausted."

"I am exhausted. But well worth it. I learned a great deal today. More than I expected to."

Jonathan offers me a cheesecake and I graciously accept. And of course it's love at first bite. Well the only bite. Bite-size literally means bite-sized.

"What do you think? About the cheesecake?" Jonathan asks, looking apprehensive and excited all at once.

"It was delicious, but I feel teased. Like I want more but know I'm only getting a bite."

He laughs, "Perfect! That's what I'm after. They are part of the Teaser Menu."

Teaser Menu? I'm really starting to think this place has some sort of a secret menu like Starbucks. Add Teaser Menu to my never-before-seen offerings here at Knight and Daze.

"Jonathan, today you've introduced me to three things that aren't mentioned anywhere on your current menu. The Wicked Salsa, the Java Man Joe coffee, and now dessert featured on a Teaser Menu I know nothing about. Can you explain why?"

Jonathan opens his mouth to speak when his cellphone rings. He glances at the caller ID as he removes the phone from the front pocket of his chef coat. He grimaces, "Shit. Hold that thought, I've gotta take this call really fast."

He excuses himself from the table and walks toward the kitchen, speaking emphatic yet inaudible words.

When he returns a few minutes later, he seems perturbed. "I'm so sorry but I have to leave right now. I've gotta go pick up my little sister. She's supposed to work the evening shift tonight as the hostess, but—"

"I'm sorry, your little sister?" I interject out of sheer curiosity.

He backs away in an obvious hurry to leave, "Yep. Her name is Olivia. Anyway, thanks for today. I'll see you tomorrow? Around the same time?"

Jonathan disappears through the front doors of Knight and Daze leaving me...dazed.

The rude, pink-haired, gum-popping hostess, *Olivia*, is Jonathan's little sister.

Yep. Shit just got kinda real.

CHAPTER 12

*T*he next morning I am all too eager to get my butt over to Knight and Daze as early as possible, despite feeling dead tired. I stayed up half the night, pondering over a strategic game plan that will help me help Jonathan achieve his goals.

The first part of said strategy is to discover an approach that will lead Jonathan to divulge why his passion for cooking has lost its prominence. Trouble is, I don't know him well enough to make him *want* to open up to me. I suppose I could inject him with magical truth serum. But I'm fresh out of that.

The second part of my strategy is getting him to be forthcoming about his apparent—Starbucks-like—secret menu. Although I'm relatively convinced he was just about to expose this yesterday—that is before our conversation was interrupted by that phone call. The one that made him abruptly leave me hanging to pick up his little sister.

Olivia.

When I told Sebastian about this last night while the two of us were having dinner at in-PHO-tuation—a fairly new Vietnamese fusion restaurant near our loft—his unsurprising response was, "You mean the rude little shit that served you the other day? Well, ain't that some Anderson Cooper-ish style breaking news."

I hop off the subway and begin my short stroll toward Knight and Daze.

The streets and sidewalks of TriBeCa are riddled with busy New Yorkers. Some in an obvious hurry to get somewhere, while others are simply out for a morning jog, a walk to the local bodega for coffee and a bagel, or dog walkers struggling to keep unruly dogs in line. My scenic drift along Leonard St. never ceases to amaze me as I'm always enamored by the trend setting lofts. I can only dream of someday living in one of them. Just a minor problem: TriBeCa lofts have become especially pricy. And don't get me wrong; I fancy the quaint little Harlem loft I share with Sebastian. The two of us rent it at a reasonably decent price since the owner is a client of Manifique. Still, there is something about the sheer ambiance, buzz, and excitement TriBeCa seems to shed. 'You've got Caviar Dreams' is what Sebastian always tells me.

I'm caught off guard by a familiar-sounding voice bursting from a short distance behind me.

"Kennedy!"

Only, it takes a few seconds for me to conclusively realize *I'm* Kennedy. Duh.

Instinctively, I pivot my body to turn toward the voice and notice it's Jonathan, almost out of breath, sprinting to catch up with me. He looks yummy...and sweaty, but not at all dressed in any sort of restaurant attire. He's wearing grey sweatpants and a plain white T-shirt. Both articles of clothing highly accentuate his extremely chiseled physique. *Stop staring*, I dutifully tell myself. My eyes don't follow the command—can I blame them? Uh, no.

"Are you on your way to the restaurant too?" I ask as he approaches me.

Jonathan stops, takes a few deep breaths, and lifts up his T-shirt to wipe off a modest expanse of sweat glistening his forehead. Of course my eyes gravitate to the six-pack show he unknowingly displays as if it were a Macy's storefront—Jonathan's 3D showcase of *what's hot now*.

"Not just yet," he says, calling my attention and wandering eyes back to our conversation. "And you're pretty early. Again. Much earlier than yesterday, in fact. You do know, if you go to the restaurant now, you won't be able to get in." He appears to study me as if he's trying to solve an elusive equation. "And, where are your glasses?"

Shit, I left those stupid *spark of smarts* glasses at home. *Quick. Think fast.*

"Oh well, they proved to be hard to keep on my face during all of the restaurant work. I'm wearing contacts. And, I was actually on my way to the coffee shop across from the restaurant," I fib. A failed attempt at not looking foolish.

Jonathan regards me with a grin. "Come. We can have coffee. What about food? Are you hungry? I know I am. These morning jogs always get my metabolism going."

I hesitate with utmost uncertainty, "Um, come? Come where?" I survey our surroundings in search of a small diner or...something.

"To my place. It's just around the corner." He lifts his perfectly pumped arm and points to a large twelve-story building made out of brick and limestone.

A TriBeCa Loft.

"Y-you live here? In TriBeCa?" I ask, fumbling with my words as if all parts of the English language just became foreign to me.

He begins to walk toward the building and motions for me to follow. A charismatic laugh escapes him. "Yes, and I promise I won't bite."

* * *

JONATHAN'S LOFT is exquisitely tidy. Okay wait. I might as well be perfectly honest here.

It's fucking amazing.

He's disappeared upstairs for a quick shower before advising me to "Make yourself at home."

I sink into a soft leather couch positioned in the center of the ample-sized living room and take this free moment to text Sebastian. Of course.

Me: Guess who I ran into while en route to the restaurant?

Sebastian: If it's that bitchass Garrett, please tell me you sucker-punched the hell out of him so hard, he flew into the street and a school bus struck him just like one did to that salty chick in *Mean Girls*. Honestly, that scene is fascinatingly epic.

Sebastian has this flat out obsession with *Mean Girls*—so much that he created a Facebook group 'All About Mean Girls'. Incredibly, it has at least 12,000 members.

Me: No silly, I ran into Jonathan while I was walking along Leonard St. Can you believe he lives here, in *TriBeCa*? In a loft? I'm at his place now.

Sebastian: Shut the fuck up! And hold on. Where exactly is Jonathan right now?

Me: He's taking a shower.

Sebastian: FaceTime session. Pronto!

Seconds later, Sebastian and I are heavily involved in a FaceTime conversation.

"Woman, what the hell are you doing at his place? I mean, yeah, I know you mentioned you need to find a way to get dude to open up, but sleeping with him so—"

"Wait. What?" I interrupt and laugh out loud like a crazy woman. "I'm not planning on *sleeping* with him. Although he did look awfully yummy in that tight-fitting T-shirt."

"Um, you can reel that sarcasm back just a notch, sweetheart," he implores as he reviews his own image on the screen, meticulously adjusting his flashy bow tie. His swaggering maneuver makes me think he only solicits FaceTime calls when he's all too lazy to walk over to a damn mirror. "I'm being serious, Penelope."

"Shhh. It's *Ken-ne-dy*," I react, enunciating my decoy name to Sebastian as if I were his second grade teacher. "And you think I'm *not* being serious?" I lower my voice to a scant whisper. "Look, this is all totally innocent. Jonathan was jogging. I was walking. Now we're at his place. I'm sure the two of us will head to the restaurant together in a bit. It's only about a block away from here."

"Fine," Sebastian gives in, "just keep that Code of Ethics pamphlet top of mind. Page five says you can't sleep with a client until at least day three."

CHAPTER 13

*a*fter Sebastian's facetious comeback, he winks at me and blows a theatrical kiss before ending our FaceTime powwow.

I toss my iPhone into my bag and sink farther into the soft abyss-like couch, allowing my eyes to scan the room in an awe-stricken fashion. Jonathan appears to have impeccable taste—clearly evident by the way the loft is gussied up. Sure it looks like a *man* resides here, but I imagined Jonathan to live in a rugged bachelor pad with dirty socks and jeans strewn here and there, half-crushed beer cans taking a permanent residence on the coffee table, and dirty dishes scattered about. Not on your life did I fathom Jonathan to live in a trendy loft with soaring ceilings beautifully contrasted by maplewood floors, walls decorated with tasteful yet subtle artwork, and floor to ceiling windows with dynamic views. Then again, I mustn't forget, I also expected him to have greasy hair, missing teeth, and a protruding beer belly.

Feeling a tad antsy, I peel myself off the couch and begin to explore. I mean Jonathan did say "make yourself at home," right?

As I rummage around, out of the living room, through the sleek dining room equipped with a table large enough to feed a city (okay, teeny tiny exaggeration but still), a peek into a quaint powder room, and back through the living room, I finally land in the most spell-binding part of this loft—the open kitchen.

Unmistakably chef-inspired, the kitchen has two integrated refrigerators—that's right, *two* of them. There are cabinets, drawers, and counter space galore, a twelve-burner top-of-the-line gas range, two ovens (again, *two*), a wine fridge that holds fifty-four bottles of wine (yes, I just counted them all), and a pantry the size of Sebastian's, Carrie-Bradshaw-inspired, walk-in closet. If only it had a TV, I could probably *live* in a kitchen like this.

Just as I'm about to open one of the two refrigerators, Jonathan announces, "I see you've discovered my man cave,"—his tone startling.

I let out a sissy-girl scream and turn toward him. I can literally feel all of the blood in my body flood my cheeks. My guess is the expression on my face is one of a naughty kid who just got caught with her hand in a cookie jar—because that's the precise aura hovering over me right now with a jumbo caption bubble that reads—oops.

I bite my lower lip and nervously fidget, finally settling on wrapping a strand of my hair around my finger. The sight of him looking all cleaned up in dark blue slacks, a tan polo shirt that hugs his perfectly sculpted build, and stylish leather oxfords, makes my vocabulary limited to a succinct three-word reply, "Your man cave?"

He draws near, once again invading *my* personal space, even though I've made said space awkwardly cramped since I'm standing with my back up against the refrigerator. He smells sensual and clean.

No hint of cilantro this time.

"Yes, Kennedy, this is my man cave, which, by definition, just so happens to be a male retreat or sanctuary in a home, such as a specially equipped room." He delivers his cocky spiel as if he's some sort of a courtroom attorney expertly defending his case.

I stand completely unable to move, as though the lower half of my body has been buried inside a one-hundred pound cinder block. His proximity is annoying, exhilarating, and intimidating, all at once—especially since he's armed himself with that playful smirk of his—a sure fire way to make me want to—

"Excuse me please," Jonathan softly asserts, cutting through my disorderly thoughts as he gently eases past my shoulder to open the refrigerator door. "You're hungry, right? That's why you're in here... you're planning to prepare us a morning feast?"

Thankfully, the lower half of my body makes an escape from the fictive cinder block and I graciously step aside. "Me cook?" I frantically shake my head from side to side. "Um, no. I'm actually cooking impaired."

Jonathan removes a carton of eggs, something wrapped in butcher paper, butter, fresh rosemary, and a small mason jar filled with some sort of sauce from the refrigerator. He looks at me and laughs. "Cooking impaired?" He skillfully kicks the refrigerator door closed with the back of his shoe and sets the food onto the center island countertop. "I have to say, your choice of words is intriguing. Most people would just keep it simple. Like, *I can't cook.*"

I walk over to the center island, park my butt on one of the swivel barstools, and lay my elbows on the cool marble countertop. I can feel the corner of my lip curve—something it tends to do all on its own when I'm feeling flirtatious. "Well, Jonathan, I'm not most people."

"Touché, Madam Prescott," he says, stepping over to the sink to wash his hands. "I'll prepare us a morning feast."

"Can I help?"

"No. But thanks for offering. I invited you, so please just sit and relax."

As Jonathan begins to artfully prepare our morning feast, I decide to go back to yesterday's conversation at the restaurant. I need insight in order to help produce winning results.

"Jonathan, yesterday we were chatting about your off-menu items. Do you mind if we circle back to that?" I inquire, my hands folded, resting comfortably on the counter as I prop up, in preparation for intuitive dialogue.

Jonathan shrugs his shoulders. "Sure, however, we may have to eat before we can dive into any deep conversation. My mind doesn't function that well on an empty stomach. You like steak and eggs?"

"Do I ever. The last time I had steak and eggs was ages ago. My dad used to prepare it every Sunday morning when I was younger."

He removes two petite filet mignons from the butcher paper, sprinkles both sides with salt, and places them on a wood cutting board. "Great. You'll be the first to taste my Steak and Eggs Benedict."

I ardently observe Jonathan as he slips into a culinary zone all his own—and like a rhythmic drummer, he doesn't skip a beat.

He cracks open two eggs, allowing them to ease into an egg-poaching pan—a gadget I wasn't aware existed until this moment. And while the eggs simmer, Jonathan gently lays the steaks in a sizzling frying pan, tossing in a couple of pats of butter and two sprigs of the fresh rosemary to boot. Next, he empties the contents of the mason jar into a small saucepan, placing it on the stove over low heat. He flips the steaks, grabs a small wooden spoon from the drawer besides the range, and deftly bastes the heck out of the filets with rosemary-infused, melted butter. It's like watching Bobby Flay on TV—but exceedingly better. Mostly because Jonathan is that much hotter. And because I can actually *smell* the yumminess prepared before me.

Somewhere in the midst of my daydream about Jonathan vs Bobby, I must have missed when one split English muffin was plopped into the toaster, because the sound of the slices popping up makes me jump in my seat. *Stop fantasizing about his lips pressed against—*

"You alright there, Ms. Prescott?" Jonathan asks, once again intruding my borderline-smutty rumination.

I mumble yes, and try to wipe the red glow from my cheeks, embarrassed I allowed my thoughts about Jonathan to momentarily take me away from my 3D cooking show. *He doesn't know what you were thinking,* my overactive imagination assures me.

Before I know it, Jonathan has expertly plated our morning feast of Steak and Eggs Benedict.

The remarkable aroma makes my mouth water. Truthfully, this meal is almost too damn beautiful to eat—his plating technique is impeccably perfect—a food photographer's dream.

"Coffee. I promised you coffee," he remembers as he walks over to the counter above the dishwasher and grabs a container of coffee, a coffee press, and two mugs. After placing them on the counter, he prepares the coffee, and thoughtfully provides me sugar, cream, and utensils needed to dig into this breakfast delight.

"Thank you, Jonathan, everything looks and smells amazing."

He slides into the barstool next to me and a small black purse falls to the floor; he tosses it aside as if it were an utter annoyance. I dare not ask who it belongs to. It's none of my business, really. But I'll admit, I am curious.

"Thanks, I sure hope you think it tastes as good as it looks. Like I said earlier, you're the first to try my dish."

He motions for me to dig in and seems to watch me, awaiting my reaction.

I slice a bite of all the elements and slide it off the fork and into my mouth. Ambrosial is the first word that pops into my head. The flavors of the steak, eggs, and sauce, all married together, simulate a honeymoon in my mouth. Who would have thought Steak and Eggs Benedict was even possible?

"Jonathan, it's magical," I say, digging in for another bite.

"You think so, huh?" he asks, looking pleased as he finally takes part in our morning feast.

"Yes," I assure, trying to speak with my mouth full. "What's in this sauce? It's not a typical hollandaise sauce."

"For someone who is *cooking impaired*, you have an impressive palate," he says, dodging my inquiry altogether.

"Well, I do eat out a lot."

He smiles, but that smile fades away quickly. I take this moment to probe again, taking full advantage of his vulnerability.

"Jonathan, as I observed you prepare this elaborate meal, you clearly demonstrate a passion for cooking," I begin, as I take small bites of my breakfast, savoring each as though it were my last, "yet, you mentioned the other day, you're not as passionate as you once were. Why is that?"

Jonathan lifts the mug full of coffee to his mouth and takes a sip. I stare at him solicitously, patiently waiting for a response.

Is this the moment when I get to delve deeper into the mystery of Jonathan Knight?

He turns to face me, takes a deep breath in and out. "I haven't had time for much of anything for the past few years." He takes another sip of coffee before placing the mug back onto the counter. "I've been trying to keep my head *and* the restaurant above water."

He looks down at his plate and pushes it aside as if this subject matter has made him lose his appetite. Part of me wants to halt my efforts at uncovering the details because I can sense Jonathan's discomposure. But this NYU trained journalist turned restaurant consultant must do what she does best. Gather information.

"If you don't mind me asking, what's happened over the past few years? Something significant that would cause your passion to be placed on hold?"

He sits still for a few seconds as if he's allowing my question to come to a simmer before providing an answer. I wait, and silently pray that what he is hopefully about to share, has nothing at all to do with my restaurant review.

He clenches one fist and places it to his mouth as he clears his throat. "Our parents died three years ago. A small private plane crash off the coast of Virginia. They were off to Florida for a weekend getaway because they had been working their fucking asses off at the restaurant—which was their third child, so to speak. It was their first vacation in years, and they never made it. Their will named me as the restaurant's successor, and I was also left to take care of my younger sister, Olivia, who at the time was only fourteen years old." He turns to face me with a poignant glare. "So yes, Kennedy Prescott. I would say something *extremely* significant has caused me to place my passion for cooking on hold."

Jonathan's revelation punctures my open wound—I know and understand all too well how it feels to suffer a loss so painfully devastating.

I struggle to hold back a floodgate of empathy-laced tears, and all I can manage to mutter in this drastically frail moment is, "I am so very sorry."

CHAPTER 14

*A*n unbreakable silence pollutes the atmosphere as Jonathan and I sit in our respective barstools, side by side, lost in our own reflective thoughts.

I so badly want to reach over and embrace him—show him how much I understand.

But I can't move.

I can hear Jonathan's intense breathing while my head saturates with headline-like flashes of potential icebreaker verbiage—none of which can cool down the torrid mood my steadfast probing has generated.

So you just had to keep probing, huh?

Ugh.

Sometimes my conscience is a Captain Obvious sarcastic bitch.

"I lost my parents too," I finally manage to murmur as I slowly trace the rim of my coffee mug with the tip of my index finger. I turn to face Jonathan and try to survey his disposition before I continue, "It happened a year ago, in fact. Car accident. My world was—*is* shattered. I have moments when I daydream their absence is nonexistent, I listen to saved voice messages the two of them left on my phone over the years, and a simple trip to the bank freaks me out, because money I inherited from the tragedy is a dismal reminder," I reveal.

Jonathan lets out a deep breath, as if relieved, and turns to face me. His eyes, once ominous, are now calm and forgiving. "Kennedy, I'm sorry. I-I honestly had no idea. And you get it. You understand." he says, his voice slightly broken.

I nod in agreement as I am faced with a sudden loss of words.

"I really haven't given myself time to grieve," he admits, rising up from the barstool to begin the task of breakfast dishes clean up. "My focus has been the restaurant and Olivia, who has good days and bad days. I thought including her in the restaurant would be good for her emotional recovery, but she's been quite a tool lately."

His comment about Olivia takes me back to my visit to the restaurant last week—and the unpleasant service she provided.

"Jonathan, I visited the restaurant last week. Olivia was the hostess," I begin, now assisting with the breakfast clean up.

I've been waiting for an opportune chance to speak with Jonathan about Olivia and since he's planted the seed, it may be now or never.

Jonathan looks at me, his expression curious, "Wonderful. I'd love to hear all about your visit," he says, tossing me a small dish towel, "While you and I do the dishes, of course. I'll wash, you dry?"

I nod yes, as I pick up the towel he tossed me from off the floor. I've never been good at playing catch.

"Of course. You wash. I'll dry." I smile, maneuvering my way next to him, forming our two-person dish washer / dryer assembly line, standing shoulder to shoulder—well, head to shoulder is more like it. Jonathan is much taller than I like to think I am.

"Anyway, like I mentioned, I visited last week—"

"Last week, when?" He interrupts handing me a few forks to dry.

"Thursday, I believe. It was in the afternoon. Olivia greeted me—"

"Wait," he interrupts, yet again, "what made you visit? Were you trying to assess us or something?"

"Yes, exactly. My intention was to view operations firsthand, as a visitor—not as a consultant."

"Makes perfect sense. Please, proceed," he softly demands as he passes over a mug.

His hand grazes my own during the somewhat intimate transaction and I flat out lose my train of thought.

Why the heck does he have this insatiable affect on me?

"Um, okay," I stammer, trying hard to regroup, "I walked in and Olivia—"

"Was she rude to you?" he readily interjects, once more, blocking my effort to complete a sentence.

Is this a bad habit of his?

"Yes, she was a bit on the unfriendly side. She seemed distracted, as if she had somewhere else to be. I felt as though I was an interruption to her day," I reveal, drying the last of our breakfast dishes.

Knowing what I know now, poor Olivia had good reason to be distracted.

With a damp towel, Jonathan wipes off the counter top in slow circular motions, as he stares pensively into thin air. It is almost like watching a slow-motion video.

Should I have waited to bring up Olivia? And what about the rest of the visit—the food, in particular? He should know about my total experience.

"You okay, Jonathan?" I ask, causing him to break loose from his thoughts.

He chucks the towel into the sink, pivots to allow his backside to lean against the counter, and stares at me with his arms expressively folded. Uncertainty beams through his darkened eyes like a crescent moon against a pitch-black sky.

"I am at my wits end when it comes to her. And I honestly don't know where to focus my efforts. Do I lay off of my seventeen-year old sister and divert my focus to the restaurant? Or do I lay off of the restaurant and focus on my sister? It's one or the other. How in the hell am I supposed to choose?"

Cautiously, I approach Jonathan, this time invading *his* personal space.

"What would your parents want you to do?" I ask, my voice low and shaky.

My simple query seems to shock our atmosphere, like a resounding sonic boom, and for a minute, I think perhaps I've crossed the line.

Who the fuck am I to dig so deep?

Jonathan looks down, avoiding eye contact, and I take his body language as a telltale sign that it's time for me to move on.

"I apologize. This is all none of my business," I say, stepping away from his personal space.

He grabs my arm, stopping me in my tracks.

"No. This *is* your business. You're here to help me, remember? I need you, Kennedy."

CHAPTER 15

"Y-you need me?" I say, feeling as though I've been thrust into a 'Rachel McAdams and Ryan Gosling type' romantic movie scene.

All Jonathan needs to do now is pull me close and kiss me long and hard.

"Well, yes. I need your *consultant* expertise," he asserts—his clarifying statement uproots me straight out of my Hollywood moment like a category-four hurricane. "I expect you to ask questions, no matter how annoying, difficult, or challenging they are for me to answer." He winks and smiles generously at me. "It's the only way to help me meet my goal."

"Right. Your goal."

Back to life, back to reality. "So then, let's return to my question... what would your parents want you to do?"

"They'd want me to make a decision that's best for everyone," he answers without reservation, taking a few steps over to the barstool, claiming his seat.

I follow and sit on the stool beside him, all agog for anything else he may divvy up.

"So, what decision is best for everyone?"

"Hell, if I know." He swivels slowly, back and forth, in the barstool. "I'm not good at this kind of shit. Did you know, before they passed away, the only role I played in the restaurant was Executive Chef? I didn't run the *entire* restaurant. We all had our roles—including Olivia." He surveys the kitchen and then quickly comes to a stand. "Come on, let's take this conversation to the living room. It's a bit more comfy in there."

He leads us to the living room, and I follow close behind him, observing the way his pants hug and draw emphasis to his firm backside.

Damn.

Since when did I become such a borderline nympho?

Jonathan motions for me to take a seat on the couch as he steps over to a towering wall cabinet, opens one of its bountiful compartments, and retrieves a large envelope. He parks himself beside me, close enough that our shoulders rub.

I decisively conclude this guy cares nothing about personal space.

He opens the envelope, peeping inside, seeming to carefully examine the contents. With a quick flip of the envelope, he begins pouring out snippets of newspaper and magazine articles that fall loosely on top of his lap.

Sifting through the papers, he begins to pass them over to me, one by one.

"Look, it's all here. Life at Knight and Daze before and after my parents died. You can see how thriving we were. A classic story of a strong family-owned business." He smiles unreservedly as he reflects. "We had a systematic method of operations—the roles I mentioned before. Mom often worked the front, always greeting and seating guests as if she were welcoming them into her own home. Dad was everywhere...the front thanking guests as they entered and exited, the bar mixing up new cocktails with the bartender, the kitchen coaching the team through busy rush periods, or in the dining room chatting with guests, easily striking up all sorts of amusing conversation. The two of them also did the hiring, firing, scheduling, payroll, etcetera. They *ran* the business. I took on the role of Executive Chef right after

I came back from culinarily school, and Olivia worked weekends alongside Mom in the front."

He leans his head back and shuts his eyes, as if doing so will be the sturdy roadblock needed to jam a barrage of tears.

I divert my attention to the selection of articles, many of which showcase Knight and Daze's delectable menu, elaborate service, 'best of' awards, and five-star ratings from worthy critics. There is even a feature magazine article on Jonathan himself with the headline that reads *TriBeCa's Sexiest Executive Chef Stirs Up The Heat In The Kitchen*.

I sift through more articles and come across one with a picture of a man and woman standing arm in arm in front of Knight and Daze. The gut wrenching headline—*Max And Sadie Knight, Owners Of Knight And Daze Grill And Bar, Killed In A Tragic Plane Crash*. The article is an in-depth summary about how the two of them opened the restaurant, determined to share their love of food and passion for serving the community they'd grown to cherish. In the beginning, Max was the head chef, dazzling patrons with an array of gourmet-inspired dishes, while Sadie's comfort zone was that of main hostess, charming folks with her charismatic and magnetic personality. It notes the many successes the restaurant had over the years, recognizes celebrities who frequently ate there, and at the end, announces Jonathan as the restaurant's new owner.

And then there is the article dated a little over two years later, straight out of the *Hudson News Bee* written by none other than yours truly. Headline: *Knight and Daze Grill And Bar - My Less Than To Be Desired Encounter*.

I try to hide it amongst the others before Jonathan spots I've come across it, but I'm not at all quick enough.

Shit.

I brace myself for the absolute worst.

"Oh yes, you've discovered the all too infamous, kick-me-in-the-nuts and leave me to die, restaurant review." He releases a sinister chuckle. "I haven't read that crapshoot since the day my sous chef ran into my office simply mortified at the shit-fest, that woman, Penelope Monroe wrote."

He grabs a hold of the review, scanning over it briefly while I watch his mood switch from calm to highly agitated.

"Would you like to read it?"

"No thank you," I say, my voice low, accurately mimicking how I feel right about now.

"I wish I had never read it," he mumbles under his breath, crumbling the article into a ball, tossing it to the floor just a few inches away from the couch. "Mind if I share something with you?" he asks, unexpectedly.

"Not at all."

"The truth is, she was right. Every damn word Penelope Monroe wrote in that scathing review was undeniably accurate. It took me a long time to be able to finally admit that."

His confession is a hard pill to swallow, and as I wait for it to completely digest, I can't help but wonder how or why he could hate someone he just admitted was right all along.

"Well, if she was so right, why do you hate her?"

He scoffs, "Well, it's pretty simple, Kennedy. I hate her because she told the whole *world* how fucked-up my restaurant was. I felt defenseless, like a tough kid knocked down by a ruthless bully—all captured on a stupid-ass video gone viral." He shakes his head and runs his fingers through his hair. "You see, I knew the restaurant was in trouble. Sales were declining, employee morale was low, and I couldn't keep up with the competition."

He gets up and walks over to one of the floor-to-ceiling windows, and continues to divulge, seeming to be scanning the prodigious view, with his hands resting in his pants pockets.

"It took time for me to learn the ins and outs of what my parents did and, in that process, I discovered the restaurant was not as profitable as it should have been. The two were barely breaking even. I wanted to hire a manager and another chef, and put time and effort into revitalizing the menu. But the money just wasn't there."

He turns back and makes his way back to the couch, finding his place next to me again.

"So, I dipped into some of the inheritance which allowed me the capital needed to hire another chef, a manager, and a few more employees. I trained them all myself. Business definitely began to pick up. Late nights, I started to play with new menu concepts—some of which I introduced you to yesterday." He looks at me and smiles, going silent, seeming to gather his thoughts.

He reaches down, retrieving the crumbled article he had earlier tossed to the floor. "Then, this happened. This ugly-truth review. And the timing could not have been worse. My inclining sales went on a swift decline and I began to slowly go into debt. I was out of dough because I couldn't dip into money I set aside for Olivia's college fund. She needs to go to college. She's got her heart set on becoming some sort of journalist."

"A journalist? No interest in delving into the family restaurant business, huh?" I ask, even though, during my brief encounter, it was blatantly obvious Olivia takes little to no interest in the family business.

"Nope. No interest at all. Frankly, I don't blame her. She needs to get out on her own—find herself and what life has to offer inside the realm of her own interests. As it is now, it's a struggle to keep her engaged and focused long enough to get her through high school."

I sit back and watch Jonathan as he morphs into this noticeably vulnerable man and realize it has to be an arduous task for him to share all of this with me—a mere outsider looking in.

He steals a glance at his watch and jumps up, grabbing my hand in his.

"Come on, time got away from me. We've got to head to the restaurant. Employees and perhaps vendors are probably waiting for me."

CHAPTER 16

he short walk from Jonathan's loft to the restaurant is filled
with effervescent small talk centered around the weather,
public transportation, and puppies...anything to eschew a horrifically
awkward silence.

By the time we arrive to the restaurant, a handful of employees I
recognize from yesterday, along with a few vendors, are waiting for
Jonathan.

"Sorry, guys, we simply lost track of time," Jonathan says,
unlocking the back entrance door.

Once inside I find my way to the restroom as I need to put on
the chef coat Jonathan provided yesterday. I reach into my
bag and—

Crap. I totally forgot to wash it last night. I can't possibly wear a
chef coat that looks like a raiment of toxic waste.

Ugh.

I'm starting to think I should have just stayed home today. Besides
the lack of sleep last night, I'm feeling pretty lousy about things
Jonathan spoke about today. Perhaps, it's not at all too late to go
home? I mean, I could very well come up with a highly credible excuse
like an onset of stomach flu, a sore throat, or even the mumps

although mumps would be far less convincing than the other two cop-outs.

Stop being a whiny diva and get out there and tell Jonathan you need another chef coat. There. Problem brilliantly solved.

And…there goes Captain Obvious, making an unwelcome appearance…again.

Just as I make my way from the restroom toward the kitchen to locate Jonathan, my eye catches him sitting in one of the booths. He appears to be on the phone, involved in a heavy conversation—only perceptible by the grumpy expression that's taken over his face, albeit momentarily, I hope.

Would walking over and sitting next to him until he ends his call be overly intrusive?

Probably.

But, not likely more of an intrusion than I was while at his loft earlier.

As I get closer, Jonathan ends his call and stands.

"Hi," I say with a hesitant smile. "Sorry to, uh, bug you, but I sort of forgot to wash the chef coat you gave me yesterday and it's extremely—"

"I have to leave," he gruffly announces, pacing back and forth as if he's trying to bring calm to his nerves.

"I'm sorry, um, leave? We just got here."

"Yeah. Well, you can come with me if you'd like. In fact, it's best if you *do* come with me. It'll give us more time to talk about the business and my goals."

I stare at Jonathan, confused.

"Go with you where, exactly?" I ask, deciding it is a reasonable question.

"Back to my place to pick up the black purse Olivia left there, then take a ride up to The Island to give it to her."

I do remember seeing the black purse today at his loft. I totally theorized it belonged to a girlfriend, assuming he probably has several of them.

Several girlfriends. Not purses.

"The Island, as in Long Island?"

"Yep. Long Island. Olivia's at my aunt and uncle's house at the moment—look, I can explain everything later. Are you coming with me or not?" he asks, with his eyes fixed on mine.

I look around the restaurant and decide I'd be lost here on my own —without him. I could go home, and risk missing out on the chance to learn more details about Jonathan—to help with his restaurant image improvement goals, of course.

"Yes, I'd be happy to join you."

"Great. Let's go," he says, looking thoroughly pleased.

Back at his place, he grabs the purse and hands it over to me. "Can you hold on to this for a sec? I need to change my clothes," he explains, headed toward the stairs.

"Sure. And uh, you look fine in what you have on," I say, hoping he doesn't think I mean that in a flirtatious way.

He laughs softly, and I watch him peel off his shirt like it's edible candy, as he reaches the top of the steps—even his back looks perfectly toned and sculpted. Like the type of chiseled yumminess I've seen on late-night workout DVD informercials that Sebastian and I sometimes watch. "Thanks, but I like to be comfortable for the ride to Long Island," he says before disappearing from sight.

He returns, wearing dark blue jeans, a black T-shirt, and plain white socks. In other words, he looks pretty damn hot.

"You ready?" he asks, flashing a smile that's fit for an Orbits' gum commercial.

"Sure am. But what about your shoes?"

"Oh. They're in the garage...Ms. Nothing Gets By Me." His sarcastic bite is irritating and alluring all at once and when he blatantly winks as he slowly walks past me, I can't help but conclude he's actually flirting with me.

"Come on, the garage is right through this door." He directs, motioning for me to follow.

I step down into the garage that is lightly illuminated by three small garage door windows, as Jonathan kindly holds the door open for me. After opening a narrow cupboard, he removes a pair of black boots and a small black German-style half helmet that he passes to me.

Wait. A helmet?

"Whoa, whoa, whoa. What the hell is this?"

"It's a helmet, Ms. Prescott. Have you never laid eyes on one before? Perhaps you should get out more."

"Of course I've laid eyes on—never mind. What I mean is why are you giving this to me?"

"Well, I'm a law-abiding man. The state of New York requires a helmet be worn by motorcycle rider...and passenger."

His sarcasm is annoyingly...hot.

"Wait. You have a motorcycle? We're going to Long Island by *motorcycle?*"

"Yep. I hate Uber and I sold my car last year, downsizing to my Harley."

He briefly passes a coy expression to me while flashing that smirky smile before he pushes a button on the wall, signaling the garage door to roll open. He pulls on his boots, one white sock-covered foot at a time, and I stand here, helmet in hand, not knowing what to do.

Sure, a ride on the back of a hot guy's Harley sounds fascinating, to say the least. But I've never in my life been on a motorcycle and I am a tad uneasy about it.

Jonathan approaches, removes the helmet from my hand, positions it on top of my head, and fastens the strap. "It looks like it was made for you," he renders in a spine-tingling tone that causes me to shiver like when I first dip my foot into a cold swimming pool, or when I heard his voice for the first time...just yesterday.

He captures my hand in his, guiding me around the corner of the spacious garage, and I stop, feeling suddenly compelled to admit I'm scared.

"Jonathan, I-I've never been on a bike before."

"Oh, a motor virgin?" His eyebrows raise, showing off his instant gratification. "Well, isn't that special? Ms. Prescott, I'd be honored to be your first; in fact, I promise to ensure your first ride will be the best ride of your life," he says, pulling me along over to his Harley.

Is it just me who detects a sexual connotation in his smutty remark?

Seeing the bike up close, in its breathtaking ride-til-you-die glory, along with Jonathan's *'best ride of your life'* articulation, resisting the urge to go along for the ride becomes downright impossible.

CHAPTER 17

*T*wenty minutes later, after crossing the Willie B, the two of us are riding fast and free, and for the first time, I understand why women swoon over a sex pistol of a man on a motorcycle—right now, my swoon level is on high alert.

With my eyes closed, arms wrapped and fingers locked securely around Jonathan's waist, and the side of my face pressed against his shoulder blade, I inhale Jonathan's enthralling masculine scent.

Why does he have this bewitching affect on me?

"Ms. Prescott, did you just take a long whiff of my T-shirt?" he asks and I thank God he is unable to catch the embarrassment flowing all over my face.

I raise my head and position my chin comfortably on the edge of his shoulder, "Um, no... Why would I take a whiff of your T-shirt? I was merely *sniffing*. Allergy season, you know."

He cocks his head to the side and I can see the corner of his mouth curl up into a flirtatious smirk. "Sure. Allergies."

I try to fight it, yet can't help but beam, feeling like a high school cheerleader who finally got noticed by the star athlete at the homecoming game.

You better stop liking him so much. You know he loathes the real you.

I tell my bubble-bursting conscience to shut the fuck up and insist she takes the next century off.

"Do you have a boyfriend, Ms. Prescott?"

His blatant question catches me completely off-guard.

"Me? A boyfriend? Uh, not anymore. I caught him cheating."

"Bastard."

"I know, right?" I roll my eyes as I free myself from the thought of Garrett. "And what about you?"

"Me? A boyfriend? Uh—"

"You know what I mean," I cut him off before he can complete his satirical response.

He chuckles. "Ok, the answer is, no. I don't have a girlfriend. Truth is I haven't had one in two and a half years.

"Really?" I ask, finding it hard to imagine a man as handsome as he staying single for that long.

Maybe he is the player I pegged him to be...

"Yep. Two and a half *long* years. She broke my heart, leaving me for another man right after my parents died."

...Or maybe he's not a player at all.

"Bitch," I spill out, not meaning to recite my thoughts.

"I know, right?" He laughs, seeming to find amusement in my candidness.

We ride over a bump and the force pushes me closer into him, and my natural instinct causes me to hold onto him that much tighter.

"Relax, Ms. Prescott, I've got you. Besides, I promised you the ride of your life. You're in good hands with me."

Somehow I believe his proclamation to be satisfyingly true.

"So why the sudden curiosity in my single or not-single status?" I ask straight out, eager to know his response.

"Sudden curiosity? What makes you think I hadn't wondered since the first day we met?"

"Oh, you mean since yesterday, right? Because we only met yesterday."

"I know. But for some reason, I feel as though I've known you for a little longer than just a day."

"You do realize that sounds like a cheesy pickup line, right?"

"Says the woman I picked up in a restaurant a little over an hour ago, who now sits on the back of my bike, taking long whiffs of my T-shirt."

I punch him lightly in the stomach and he lets out a playful yelp.

A talkfest about the Harley—in which Jonathan tenderly refers to as *The Beast*—the panoramic ride, and how he is a New York native, steals time and before I know it we pass a sign that says, *Welcome to East Hampton.*

The Hamptons?

"So…when you said we were gonna ride to Long Island, you failed to say you actually meant The Hamptons?" I ask, as I covertly squeal and do a mental happy dance. I've never been to The Hamptons. But I've always wanted to go.

It's on my Cinderella list.

"Oh, yeah, surprise! Uncle Joe and Aunt Becca live here in East Hampton. They've run a popular bed and breakfast for the past fifteen years. Well, Aunt Becca is the one who runs it. Uncle Joe spends three days a week away from home. He's a commercial airline pilot. It's been a few months since I've been back. I love it here," he says as we slowly ride past quaint little shops and Mom-and-Pop style restaurants.

"I've never been here," I softly admit, taking in the East Hampton breeze.

"Another first for you, huh? Now I wonder how many firsts we can check off your list today, Ms. Prescott?"

Jonathan throttles The Beast as we turn a sharp corner. By now, I am totally trusting of the way he handles the bike—with authoritative gentleness. Something deep in my gut makes me wonder if he handles his woman with the same consideration.

With another swift turn, we end up on Main Street slowing to a cruising speed. Just ahead, I spot a charming two-story colonial with a sign that reads *Brier Hill Manor.*

Jonathan rides up the elongated driveway, and brings the bike to a halt, lowering his boots to the ground.

He shuts off the motor and lowers the kickstand. "Here we are: Brier Hill."

Jonathan eases off of the bike, then takes my hand to safely guide me off. I remove my helmet, handing it to Jonathan, my eyes fixated on the gorgeous manor.

"Wanna take a look inside?" he asks.

"Does a margarita need good tequila?" I jokingly reply. "Of course I wanna look inside."

He grabs my hand, leading me up a brick walkway, then up four steps and onto a covered wraparound front porch that's outfitted with cushioned rocking chairs—one red, one white, and the other blue—and matching side tables.

"Now let me warn you, my Aunt Becca is—"

"Jonathan, darlin'," a woman's voice says as we approach the front door.

The screen door swings open and out prances a petite older woman who has a bright smile, about a mile long. She's casually dressed in tan crop pants, a denim long-sleeve button-down blouse, sandals, and a red-and-white checkered apron.

Jonathan produces a mighty grin, tightly embracing who I can only guess is his aunt.

"Hi, Aunt Becca; as always, you look like you just stepped out of *Vanity Fair* magazine."

She blushes, her hands frenziedly patting the sides of her dark brown hair that's tastefully secured in a classic Audrey-Hepburn-style bun. "Oh Jonathan, you can charm the socks and shoes off anyone."

She looks at me with her ocean-blue eyes and smiles curiously.

"Oh sorry, Aunt Becca, this is Kennedy Prescott," Jonathan mentions.

I extend my hand for a handshake and she swoops in for a hug.

"I'm a hugger, darlin'" she says, still holding onto me tightly. She breaks away and adds, "You, my dear, are quite a beauty, Kennedy."

Jonathan shakes his head, raking all ten of his fingers through his hair.

"Kennedy is a Restaurant Consultant, Aunt Becca. She's helping me with a project," he claims with his voice a bit shaken.

"Oh I see," says Aunt Becca with furrowed brows, looking slightly disappointed. She wipes her hands on her apron, "Well, anyway, let's get you two inside. Your timing couldn't have been better. I just pulled a batch of sugar cookies out of the oven."

CHAPTER 18

I was dead wrong.

When I first laid eyes on Jonathan's state-of-the-art kitchen, I thought it rightfully deserved the nickname: kitchen badass.

Until now.

As I sit at the center island breakfast bar (which is massively sized), surveying every single detail of this kitchen—shrine, I realize *this* is the most badass kitchen I've ever stepped foot in.

Aunt Becca is serving me up scrumptious sugar cookies and tea while Jonathan excused himself to retrieve Olivia's purse and a few other items he stored in the storage compartment of The Beast for the ride up here.

"It's so darn good to have Jonathan home," Aunt Becca says cheerfully, as she pours me hot tea from a tea kettle into a matching blue-and-yellow floral teacup. She speaks softly, with a scant southern drawl.

"Home?"

"Why, yes. Jonathan lived here with us, off and on, as a teenager. He was quite the young rebel back then," she says, offering me a small bowl of sugar cubes.

"A rebel, huh?" I ask, fully amused, plopping two sugar cubes, one after another, into the steaming cup of tea.

She walks around the center island, taking a seat next to me on what appears to be a custom-made double bar stool. She taps her fingers on the counter, as she turns to face me.

"Yep. We all go through our rebel years and Jonathan was no exception. So, my sister-in-law Sadie and my older brother Max, God rest their beautiful souls, sent him here every summer. My husband Joe and I would put him right to work. My momma always told me you've gotta work hard in order to remain humble."

I take a sip of tea and grin. "Well, your momma sounds like a smart woman. So, what sort of work did you two make Jonathan do?"

She shrugs her shoulders. "We placed him wherever we needed help. First, it was cleaning guest rooms, then it was groundskeeper, and then it was kitchen duty. And that's when we all began to see a significant shift in his attitude. It was like watching a mind-blowing metamorphosis. He—well, we all—recognized cooking and food as his passion."

"Wait. So right here is where it all began?" I ask, my mouth full of a bite of the fresh-baked sugar cookie. I can't help but smile at the thought of a young, stubborn Jonathan, working out his frustrations in the kitchen.

"Yep. In this very room." She takes a deep breath, surveying the entire room. "Well, it has changed ever so slightly over the years. Particularly the size. It used to be quite small, but Jonathan had this idea to knock out a wall that once separated the large dining room and the small kitchen. We hired a contractor—and presto."

I nod, trying to picture the kitchen at a much smaller scale.

"So," begins Aunt Becca, "how long have you known Jonathan?"

"Not that long, Aunt Becca," Jonathan interjects as he re-enters the kitchen, carrying Olivia's purse, my bag, and his backpack. He eyeballs me briefly, then winks.

"I was just hearing all about your rebel stage, Jonathan." I smile at Aunt Becca, as she gets up and prepares a plate of cookies for Jonathan.

"Oh yeah? Well, I guess I was quite the teenager. And now it's Olivia's turn to rebel out." He looks at his watch. "Where is she anyway?"

Aunt Becca places a plate of cookies on the counter next to my plate and Jonathan glides into the double barstool right next to me.

I no longer mind him taking refuge in my personal space. I've grown to expect it now.

"She's at her friend Daphne's house and your uncle is going to bring her back here tomorrow when he gets back from Seattle." Aunt Becca rubs the back of Jonathan's hand, "You've gotta relax, honey. Olivia is going to be just fine here. After all, look what this town did for you."

Jonathan cups his hand over hers. "I know, Aunt Becca. That's why I sent her here. But, she left her purse with her phone in it, so here I am...dutifully dropping it off."

Aunt Becca smiles at Jonathan, then quickly turns to me.

"And you decided to accompany him for the ride up here, hun?"

I feel my cheeks heat up as I can't help but think Aunt Becca is trying to get the scoop on Jonathan and me...only there is absolutely nothing to scoop. However, I have to admit, sitting behind him on that bike, with my arms wrapped so intimately around his body, there were a few moments when I daydreamed the two of us—

"I invited her to come along so we could discuss business, Aunt Becca," Jonathan answers, interrupting my heavy-heated runaway train of thought.

"I see." She gleams and the look in her eyes reveals she has more suspect opinions about the matter. "You should take Kennedy on a tour of Brier Hill," Aunt Becca suggests as she cleans up our teacups and cookie plates. "Don't mind me... I have menu items to prepare for this weekend."

Jonathan agrees to take me on a tour, and takes my hand, helping me off the stool. He hands over my bag and Olivia's purse, then swings his backpack strap over his shoulder.

"Thank you for the delicious cookies," I say, as Jonathan strings me along.

"Anytime darlin'. Anytime."

As we exit the kitchen, Jonathan leads the way through a long hallway that has baby blue walls. I notice the black and white pictures hanging, showcasing town events over the years.

We approach a spiral staircase and Jonathan says, "How about we start your tour upstairs, Ms. Prescott?"

"Uh, sure," I say, realizing he still has my hand in his—and I dare not cut myself loose. I'm giddy about the way my hand fits perfectly in his.

Once upstairs, we drop off Olivia's purse in her room. Jonathan guides me through the library, shows me numerous guest rooms, and briefly shows me his room. Then we walk back downstairs, out through the front screen door, and through the expansive backyard, where he shows me a tennis court, a greenhouse, a breathtaking garden courtyard, and an outdoor kitchen.

The grounds are gorgeous and more beautiful than any article I've ever read about Hampton homes and inns.

"So, since you've never been to The Hamptons, would you like to tour the town with me? I'd love to take you to see one of my favorite spots."

"Of course. But what about Knight and Daze? Shouldn't we get back?"

"They are fine. I overstaffed this week so I could take time off from the restaurant floor to spend time with you, there, or anywhere else we can execute a plan."

"Well then, I guess we are all set," I say, feeling my giddy alert rise.

"Come on. We can walk."

Jonathan makes an excellent tour guide as we roam the streets of downtown East Hampton. I've learned about some local history and we even stopped a few times, chatting with store patrons who have known Jonathan since he was little. Now famished, Jonathan takes me into a cute little diner called Just Eat, right off Main Street.

The waitress seats us in a booth in the far corner of the restaurant. I slide in and Jonathan follows, plopping down right beside me—I don't even waste my brainpower trying to ascertain why he chose to sit next to me, instead of across from me.

"Sorry about my Aunt Becca," he says after the waitress takes our order. "She's annoyingly snoopy about my love life, as I'm sure you gathered. I tried to warn you, but then she barged out of the house before I had the chance."

"No worries. She seems sweet, and I can tell she cares a great deal about you."

Jonathan takes a sip of water. "Yep. Uncle Joe and her are like a second set of parents. They always have been, even before Mom and Dad died."

"It's great that you have them."

"I know, and I'm grateful they are taking in Olivia for the rest of the summer. It will give her time away from the city and the restaurant."

Jonathan looks down as if he's in deep thought, and I wonder if we hadn't left his loft for the restaurant this morning, would he have opened up, revealing more about his goals, his hopes, or even his dreams?

He turns to look at me, his eyes pensive. "Kennedy, can I share something with you, without judgment?"

"Of course," I say, shifting into a more comfortable position.

"Back at my loft, you asked me what would be the best decision for everyone, when it comes to Knight and Daze."

I nod forcefully in agreement as I take slow sips of water.

"Truth is, I sometimes think the best thing would be for me to sell it."

"Sell it?" I repeat, slightly taken aback.

"Yes. Don't get me wrong; I'm all for legacies, but honestly, walking in there every single day breaks my fucking heart. It's like a never-ending reminder that they are no longer here. And I thought it would get easier as the years go by. But it's not. And all of that coupled with the break-the-bank issues—running that restaurant has become a hindrance. And I hate myself for feeling this way."

He sinks his face into the palms of his hands, clearly frustrated.

I place my hand on his thigh, "It's okay, I understand. You mustn't hate yourself for feeling the way you do. But you do need to do what's in your heart. You know deep down, your parents would want you and Olivia to be happy. And doing what you have to do to achieve that, shouldn't make you feel guilty, Jonathan."

Saying that aloud makes me think about myself and the issue I have with the money in the bank. I want to spend it, but feel so guilty spending money received because of their death. How am I supposed to look at it as a benefit?

The waitress drops off our plates. We both ordered the Chef's Salad.

"If you decide to sell, what would you do? What will Olivia do?" I ask, in between two small bites of salad.

Jonathan wipes his mouth with a napkin. "Well, after I pay off bills and debt, I'd set up most of the money from the sell in a trust for Olivia, sell my loft, and move here."

"Here? To the Hamptons?" I say, my eyes wide in amusement.

He chuckles slightly. "Yes. I mentioned before, I love it here. I dream of buying a modest home near the water and opening a small restaurant in town. Olivia would live with Uncle Joe and Aunt Becca, while she finishes high school. They have an excellent journalism program there. She's already researched it."

His face lights up at his revelation and, even though I've known him for only a little over twenty-four hours, I haven't seen him glow like this since this morning, when he was preparing our Steak and Eggs Benedict.

"What's stopping you?"

"Good question. How about Guilt? Fear? Uncertainty?" He shrugs his shoulders. "Lack of self-confidence? You name it."

"Sometimes we use excuses as a crutch that holds us back."

"Or sometimes excuses prevents us from making a horrible mistake."

I push my food around the plate, too engrossed in our conversation to eat.

Jonathan seems to notice. "Not that hungry either, huh?"

"Not really," I confess.

"Great, then let's go. I'd love to show you something."

Jonathan pays for our meal and we head back out to explore more of the Hamptons.

"So, I've toyed with the thought of selling for about a year now," he says, as we walk along Main Street. "And I ran it across my aunt and uncle about six months ago."

"And?"

"And, like you, they told me to follow my heart. Seems like no one will come out and tell me it's a good or a bad idea."

"Right. Well, it doesn't really matter what anyone else thinks, does it?"

He smiles. "You're quite sassy, aren't you?"

"Not at all." I wink.

He leads the way around a corner and we walk past a few shops and restaurants, finally coming to a halt in front of a small building.

"Here we are: my favorite spot to eat."

"'Your favorite spot to eat?"

Perplexed, I stare at the building, in wonder, as it appears to be completely...empty—equipped only with a small real estate sign that says: For Lease. Contact Winfield Bank and Trust for More Information.

"Assuming it was mine, it would be my favorite place to eat," Jonathan clarifies, with that happy gleam in his eyes—a look I'm growing super fond of.

"You want to buy this place?"

"Or lease it—like the sign says." He points to the 'for lease' sign.

"Was it a restaurant at one time?"

"Yes. A bakery. The owners, who had been here for over ten years, packed up and moved their business to California four years ago. They've been trying to sell the place, but no one seems to be interested."

I move closer, leaning into the window, taking a closer peek inside. "Or maybe, it's just sitting here, waiting for Jonathan Knight to stake his claim."

"Hmm. I'm starting to like your sassafras, Kennedy Prescott."

He glances at his watch and a cool breeze blows right through us.

"We should probably head back to Brier Hill. It's getting late, and we still have to ride back into the city," he says, taking my hand.

By the time we step foot back in the manor, and into the kitchen, Aunt Becca is cooking up something that smells delectable.

"Hey, you two," she says, setting the table, "I was wondering when y'all were gonna get back. It's almost dark. You can't possibly ride home this late." She looks concerned.

"We will be fine, Aunt Becca. Especially if we leave right now," Jonathan says, offering me a glass of water.

"Oh, well I prepared meatloaf and potatoes. I'm sure you've walked up an appetite."

Aunt Becca is right. I'm starving. I never finished my salad during lunch, and the smell of her meatloaf is making my stomach growl angrily.

"Well, I am hungry," I say, looking at Jonathan, assessing his reaction.

"Okay, Aunt Becca. You win. We'll stay for dinner and then head back."

"Head back? Jonathan, you two should really consider staying the night. I'd be worried about y'all on that bike so late," she relays with high concern.

"I have no change of clothes here," I interject.

"Oh my dear, no worries. We have a shop here at the manor for tourists. Didn't Jonathan show you? It's got all kinds of clothing: pants, dresses, bathing suits, undergarments. You can pick out whatever you need. On the house, of course," she says, taking the meatloaf out of the oven. "And Jonathan has a bunch of his own clothes upstairs in his room."

Jonathan shrugs his shoulders, "I'll do whatever Kennedy feels up to. I invited her along, only to drop off the purse. I'm sure she's got her heart set on getting back to the city."

"Actually, I don't mind. So long as I have something to sleep in and a fresh set of clothes to change into in the morning," I say, thinking it may be kind of cool to stay the night in the manor. Plus, if I'm lucky, it will give me more time to continue to learn about Jonathan.

"Jonathan can take you to the shop. It's closed now, but here is the key," she says, removing a small key from her pocket, handing it over to Jonathan. "I'll finish setting up for dinner and see you two back here in about twenty minutes?"

"Sounds good, Aunt Becca," Jonathan answers.

At the shop, I pick out a pair of jeans, some socks, a Brier Hill Manor T-shirt, some panties, a toothbrush, and toothpaste. Jonathan repeatedly insists I can wear a button-down pajama shirt he never wears, so I don't bother searching for anything to sleep in. After the three of us eat dinner, chatting about Brier Hill, Aunt Becca as a little girl growing up in Virginia, how she met Uncle Joe when she was a flight attendant, and how Jonathan needs a love life, Jonathan takes me upstairs, first stopping at his room to grab the pajama shirt, before he shows me to my room.

"Well, here it is; I hope it's roomy enough for you," Jonathan says, showing me into my room. "It's got a bathroom in here. " He opens the door to the bathroom. "Oh, and your clothes from the shop." He hands me the bag of clothes I picked out.

"Thank you, Jonathan. I had a great time today."

"Me too. And I'm sorry time got away from me. But it's really your fault," he says with a smirk.

"My fault? How so?" I ask, my arms defensively folded.

"It seems I lose all track of time when I'm with you."

He's flirting.

Damn him.

And why does he have to look so hot?

Why couldn't he be the greasy-haired, toothless, brute I imagined him to be?

"Anyway, it's getting late. I'll leave you to get settled. If you need anything, I'm across the hall."

Jonathan steps out and closes the door.

And I jump into the shower to cool off.

CHAPTER 19

I decide to text Sebastian after I've showered, dressed, and made myself comfy in the queen-sized poster bed. Letting Sebastian in on my whereabouts is probably a good idea, before he freaks out and calls the National Guard to search for me.

Me: Hi!

Sebastian: Hello, stranger. Working late?

Me: Um, well, I'm actually in The Hamptons. At Brier Hill Manor —Jonathan's Aunt and Uncle run the place.

Sebastian: Say what? I'm confused.

Me: Long story, but I accompanied Jonathan (on his Harley, by the way) here to drop off Olivia's purse. We got to touring the town and then became engaged in deep conversation. Before we knew it, it was late. His aunt suggested we stay the night and ride back to the city tomorrow.

Sebastian: I knew it. You're totally going to pull your panties off for him tonight!

Me: Wrong.

Sebastian: I'm never really wrong.

Me: Look, it's totally innocent. I'm in my room. He's in his. Plus, this is all business, no pleasure.

Sebastian: Yeah, right. I bet you 36 bucks you'll end up in bed with Mr. Casanova tonight.

Me: Why 36 bucks?

Sebastian: Woman, it's been 36 hours since you first met him, and tonight your panties will come off.

Me: Have a good night, Sebastian.

Sebastian: You too, cupcake.

Fifteen minutes later, I develop a mad craving for the sugar cookies Aunt Becca provided earlier. After pacing the cold, hard wood floor for less than a minute, I convince myself to head downstairs, in search of some.

After a quick peek in the floor-length mirror, I decide the pajama shirt Jonathan let me borrow is adequate attire as its length covers my bare thighs down to my knees.

Opening the door quietly, I look to the left, then to the right.

The coast is clear.

Not a single person—namely Jonathan—in sight.

Once downstairs, I find my way to the kitchen, enter through the swinging double doors, and turn on the light.

And...after about five minutes of rummaging, the cookies are nowhere in sight.

Damn.

And they were so darn scrumptious too.

Feeling defeated, I make my way back toward the stairs and up.

As I face my bedroom door, trying hard to open it unnoticed, Jonathan opens the door to his room, which incidentally, is across from mine.

I freeze, unable to either open my door and run in, or turn around and face Jonathan.

"Ms. Prescott? Are you alright?"

I nod yes, unable to speak.

I don't even want to look at Jonathan because—well because I don't want to pay Sebastian thirty-six bucks.

"Was that you I heard a few minutes ago? Were you looking for something?" he says, sounding as though he's chewing on something.

"Cookies. I was searching for cookies," I say, my back still facing him.

"These cookies?" he says, and I immediately turn around to find Jonathan holding a plate full of cookies.

"Yes! Those cookies. May I have some?"

"Sure, you can." He walks toward me, then pauses, holding back the plate, as if it's some sort of bargaining chip. "You wanna join me for a bit? My room is pretty large. Plus I have Netflix. We can stream a movie."

My contemplative eyes switch between the plate of cookies and the innocent look on Jonathan's face, and I make up my mind.

I want cookies.

And a movie.

Jonathan's room is impressively larger with a huge 50-inch TV, a king-sized bed, a cozy electric fireplace, and a sofa / love seat combo.

"Where would you like to sit? The bed or the sofa?" he asks, seeming to want me to feel comfortable and at ease.

I survey the room and notice the TV is on a wall parallel to the bed. Even if I felt more comfortable on the sofa, I can't see the TV screen unless I'm on the bed.

"Well, I can only see the TV from the bed."

"Okay. Well, can I trust you on a bed next to me?" he jokingly asks.

"Absolutely not," I retort, confiscating the plate of cookies as I trolley on over to the bed.

After perusing through two dozen movies, we both settle on *Chef*, viewing it on his bed, with two pillows between us, clearly identifying his side and my side.

A few hours later, I open my eyes, quickly realizing I'd fallen asleep in the middle of the movie. I look over and see Jonathan lying on his back, looking so peaceful, fast asleep. I could probably watch him for hours, with the soft glow from the TV's blueish screen acting as the only light source, illuminating the room like a moonlit sky.

I really should get up and go back into my own room.

But I feel safe here.

Like I belong here.

Careful not to disturb him, I reach over Jonathan, to retrieve the remote control to try to turn off the TV.

And of course in doing so, his eyes open, just as my arm moves over his chest. Fail.

We stare at each other for a moment and then, without much of a warning, Jonathan lifts his head up toward mine and kisses me, his hands holding the back of my head softly but steady.

I feel hot and cold at the same time, and all I can think of is how much I *don't* want him to stop. He turns me onto my back, moving his body in-between my bare thighs, and our kissing gets deeper and more stimulating as his tongue purposefully traces my upper lip.

As his lips move down my neck, sensually kissing their way down my chest, my stomach, and to my navel, he slowly unbuttons my shirt. Chills race up and down my spine, and I can feel my breaths quicken as his mouth discovers my panties. His hands grip my breasts and he traces my nipples until they are as hard as I imagine his erection to be. His hands move from my breasts to my thighs and then covertly to my panties as I feel them being slowly pulled off.

At first, I think I need to tell him to wait, this all may be moving at the speed of light. Never in my life have I skipped from first base to... home base. But through his kisses, I've suddenly lost the ability to think straight, like someone else has taken over.

His mouth, warm and smooth, moves from my waistline to my inner thigh. He pauses, looking up at me as if waiting for me to grant him permission. I run my fingers through his hair and smile, revealing my consent. His lips continue the charitable offer of more sensational pleasure as they find my happy place, and I moan, getting lost in absolute delight. My hands move from his hair to grip the sheet beneath me, as if doing so will help me hold my body steady—but I give in as his lips, fingers, and tongue work together on a mission—a powerful threesome up against my soft—

"Oh my fucking gosh," I shout, losing myself. My body shakes and quivers as the orgasm seemingly takes over, robbing me of my sexually timid inhibition.

My first orgasm. Ever.

And it was fucking hot.

I lay underneath him, legs trembling as Jonathan's lips move unhurriedly from south to north, eventually finding my breasts, my neck, and then my open mouth.

I can feel his erection trying to escape from the opening of his pants, and he moves his mouth over to my earlobe and softly whispers, "Was that your first orgasm, Ms. Prescott?"

Was I that fucking obvious?

"Yes," I admit, feeling no shame whatsoever. I clearly doubt I'm the only woman in New York who has never had an orgasm. Right?

"Another first? I'm beyond honored, Kennedy." He kisses my neck and my mouth before saying, "I suggest you brace yourself. There is a hell of a lot more where that came from."

CHAPTER 20

*S*ome prudishly suggest a woman shouldn't hook up with a man before the two reach their third date.

And now, to that bullshit, I say why not get sex out of the way even before the *first* date? This way you'll know, in a flash, whether or not he's worth dating.

After all, there is nothing worse than investing time and sometimes money choosing all of the right outfits, enduring the senseless small talk, trenching your way through dates one, two, and three, only to discover on date four, the guy you imagined would knock your socks off in bed, is a total fucking dud.

And I haven't at all come to this grandiose epiphany because I had sex with Jonathan last night—before we've even had anything close to a third, let alone, a first date.

But, for the record, Jonathan Knight is totally worth dating. Probably worth marrying too. He unmistakably knocked my socks off, clear to California.

* * *

SUNLIGHT HASN'T QUITE MADE its entrance through the window

shades, but I know it's dawn because I can hear birds chirping in the distance. Jonathan's steady breathing and rhythmic heartbeat keep me in a lull-like trance as I lie wrapped in his arms—while he sleeps soundly. We made love several times last night...and early this morning.

Wait, did I say made love?

Typical woman, mixing feelings with sex. Which is precisely why some suggest not to hook up with a man before the third date.

I mentally give my conscience the finger—didn't I give that troll the next century off?

Although, she's sort of right. How can I not mix feelings with sex? He gave me my first orgasm...and plenty more after that. That alone is worth developing feelings for, right? I admit, Jonathan is only the third man I've ever had sex with. And compared to those before him, no other man has been selfless enough to please me first. Not even Garrett, with whom I thought I was so madly in love.

The odd thing I can't quite wrap my dizzy head around is why Jonathan has seemed to have made me groggy since I laid eyes on him. His looks? Abso-fucking-lutely. But it's far more than that. He's been the electric jolt needed to jumpstart my heart again.

Thoughts of our conversation about his goals, hopes, and dreams, roll vigorously through my mind, and I ponder ways I can help Jonathan.

Perhaps he should sell. Turn the page on the city—move onto a new chapter for him and Olivia.

But where would that leave me? Will he turn the page on me, as well?

It'll serve me right, especially since he hates the *real* me.

Regardless, I agreed to help him improve his image and reputation...even if that means helping him conclude what's best for him, his sister, and Knight and Daze.

I create a mental checklist of the pros and cons of Jonathan setting up shop here in The Hamptons, and so far, the pros list seems a lot longer. The property he showed me that's for lease seems a reasonable size for a small restaurant and, albeit business operations here undoubtedly have seasonal fluctuations, it may be easier to manage.

Jonathan shifts a bit, and I place my leg in between his, admiring the bulge I see underneath the thin sheet covering us both.

God, he's sensually fierce.

The kind of guy women read about in those racy romance novels.

He strokes my hair and I lift my head off his chest to face him.

"You're awake?" I ask.

He smiles, rolling over on top of me, now nestled in-between my legs that are perfectly straddled around him. "I had this steamy dream I made love to a beautiful woman all night long. Oh wait. I *did* make love to a beautiful woman all night long."

We kiss and the only thing I can concentrate on, before he eases himself inside of me is, he said he made love to me...

* * *

"I DON'T WANT you to think I'm a man whore," Jonathan announces, wrapping a towel around his waist after the two of us finally step out of his steam-filled bathroom. A quick shower turned into a forty-five minute nookiefest.

"A man whore?" I repeat, standing with only a towel wrapped around my head, playfully snatching the towel off him.

He lifts me up and lays me onto the bed. "Yes, a man whore. In other words, I don't want you to think I sex up any beautiful woman I just met."

I sit up, "Wait. Does that mean you think I'm a *woman* whore?"

Jonathan laughs and shakes his head, "Oh no...there is *no* way I'm thinking you're a whore." He yanks the towel off my head, gently pushes me down, and lays on top of me. "I made you cum for the first time last night" he says, lowering his voice to a hum, "and that my sweet Kennedy, is totally non-whore status. And super-fucking sexy."

CHAPTER 21

Trying not to be incredibly conspicuous, Jonathan saunters downstairs fifteen minutes before I do, in an effort to prevent Aunt Becca from jumping to any conclusions about how the two of us spent our evening.

And when I finally make my way down, I find them both in the kitchen, cooking breakfast together.

"Good morning, Kennedy! How did you sleep?" Aunt Becca asks, whisking up a bowl of eggs.

"Yeah, Kennedy, was your bed cozy enough?" Jonathan adds, one eyebrow raised, clearly being a smart-ass.

"I slept just fine, thank you," I say, looking only at Aunt Becca. "Best sleep I've had in *years*, in fact. I actually feel brand-spanking new," I add, glancing at Jonathan.

"Lovely to hear! I hope you're hungry? Breakfast will be ready in about ten minutes."

"Thank you, I'm starving," I admit.

After breakfast, Jonathan and I load up The Beast, in preparation for the ride back into the city.

In all actuality, I'm sad to leave. So far I love everything about The Hamptons, Brier Hill, Aunt Becca, and…being close to Jonathan.

I give Aunt Becca a meaningful hug goodbye.

"You are more than welcome to come back here anytime, sweetheart," she tells me, handing me a small, brown paper bag. "I baked more cookies early this morning." She winks.

I smile generously, feeling grateful to have had the opportunity to meet her.

"You ready?" Jonathan asks, grabbing a hold of my hand.

"Yep." I fib and he leans in, giving Aunt Becca a kiss on the cheek.

We climb onto the bike, and Jonathan revs up The Beast, waiting until she quiets to a purr before he backs her down the long driveway.

We ride for a only half a block, reaching the corner when Jonathan stops and lowers his boots to the ground. "Hey…" he rubs the side of my thigh, "…are you okay? You looked a little down back at Brier Hill."

He noticed, even though I tried hard to conceal it.

"Yeah, I'm okay. Are you okay?" I ask, being slightly coy.

"No. Not really." I can't tell if he's being serious or not. He grabs my hand and kisses it softly. "Come on, Ms. Prescott. Let's head to the beach. I think you and I need a little more time together before we ride back."

Main Beach is right off Ocean Avenue in East Hampton. I've read about it in vacation magazines, vowing to visit if I were ever lucky enough to step foot in The Hamptons. Thanks to Jonathan, Lady Luck is smiling down on me.

He parks The Beast and the two of us climb off, removing our helmets, both taking in the refreshing morning sea breeze.

Taking my hand in his, Jonathan leads me up a narrow path. "I've got a cool spot where I sometimes hang out, looking down at the waves, while I sit and think."

And a cool spot it is. We sit, inside of an empty lifeguard station, our legs hanging over the ledge with our eyes glued to the picture-perfect view of the ocean.

He puts his arm around me and I lean into his shoulder.

"So, what's bothering you, Ms. Prescott?"

I look up at him; he smiles and kisses my nose.

"I told you I'm fine, remember?" I keep my eyes on the crashing waves, hoping to God he doesn't keep probing.

Truth is I'm a tad emotional. Combine all that he shared yesterday about his goals and dreams with how we spent the evening, it's a lot for me to soak up.

He strokes my hair and kisses my forehead. "Well, for some reason, I'm not fine. I don't know how to explain it, Kennedy. I feel as though something is missing, like I can't get enough of you."

I turn to look at him, wondering if he means that in a sexual way.

"And I don't mean sexually, " he clarifies as if the look on my face told him exactly what I was thinking. "Although I do believe I can spend an entire week holed up in bed with you…and still crave more."

I laugh at his honesty. "So, if not sexually, what do you mean?"

"It's like you're this intoxicating stimulant that makes me do and say things I wouldn't with anyone else. Take yesterday for instance; you're the only person I've opened up to about my thoughts on the restaurant and my desire to open up something here. You and I are the only two on earth who know that side of me. And then last night. Believe me, when I invited you in my room, the last thing I planned to do was make love to you—even though I pretty much surmised how hot you are the day I saw you standing over my desk in my office— which, of course, was only two days ago. And yes, Kennedy, I made love to you—it was more than just sex to me. Still, being that close to you, mentally and physically, I feel like I can't seem to get enough of you. You're like a damn drug."

He takes a hold of my chin, turning my face to his, and deep within those hypnotically alluring blue eyes, I detect pure veracity.

We kiss, with the sound of waves crashing in the background like a stadium of spectators cheering us on.

And when our lips finally unlock, he says, "So, are you going to tell me what's on your mind? I know you said you're okay, but I don't think so."

"Jonathan, I really think you should give The Hamptons a chance —a dry run, if you will."

He shrugs. "I'd love to, but I have no idea where to begin."

"Right. Well I gave it some thought this morning, while you were sleeping. Have you ever heard of a Pop-up restaurant?"

"I have, sort of," he says, unsure.

"Well, they are temporary restaurants—a fabulously ingenious way to provide a glimpse of what your permanent restaurant will be like. Think of it as speed dating: you and your potential client base can learn about each other in a short amount of time and ultimately determine if you're a fit."

His eyes widen, and he brushes the hair from my eyes as a small wind gust blows past us. "It certainly sounds intriguing. You think I should try this Pop-up concept? And if so, when and where?"

"How about now...well at least this weekend, at the place you showed me yesterday? I mean, we're already here. And maybe not by happenstance."

"You mean lease the space for the weekend?"

"It will probably have to be for a few days before you open for the weekend...you know, to set up and everything."

"Winfield Bank and Trust are the leaseholders, according to the sign," Jonathan says, his mood shifting to bothered.

"Right. Is there something wrong?"

"I'm not sure they will grant me anything. Seems I've lost whatever status I had with them, when I fell behind on some payments last year."

I rub my hands across his firm chest and kiss him softly.

"Don't you worry about them. I know the Winfield family extremely well."

CHAPTER 22

*R*iding around with Jonathan in The Hamptons produces a mighty feeling of exhilaration, intimidation, and captivation all bundled up in a ball lodged somewhere between my heart and my gut.

I keep kicking myself mentally, for not visiting sooner; although, ending up here with Jonathan has proven, so far, to be serendipitous, in many more ways than one.

Much like he shared with me, I too feel like I can't get enough of him. The realization scares me—I haven't felt like this for a man, ever.

We turn on Main Street and Jonathan pulls in front of the empty building up for lease, rolling to a stop.

"You up for this, Ms. Prescott? I'm gonna need your help from start to finish."

I lean in, still straddling him as I nestle behind him on the bike. "You bet I'm up for this. Can't think of anywhere else I'd rather be."

He grabs his cell phone and calls the phone number listed on the sign in the window to request an appointment to view the building's interior.

"They'll be able to meet us here in two hours," he says, looking at his watch.

"That's fine. What shall we do until then?"

He smiles curtly, puts his helmet over his head and says, "I've got just the place for us; hold on tight, pretty lady."

We end up at Herrick Park, comfortably settled under a tree, after stopping at a local supermarket for picnic fixings: pasta salad, cheese, crackers, grapes, plastic goblets, white wine, and a small blanket.

How I got so lucky, I don't know. I'm expecting this Cinderella experience to be cut off anytime now. Jonathan's bike is sure to mysteriously change into a pumpkin sometime during our duration here.

"Kennedy Prescott, you've learned a great deal about me over the past couple of days. Let's say you share a little about yourself?" Jonathan says, pouring us both half-filled goblets of wine.

Yeah, like how your real *name is not Kennedy Prescott?* My conscience resurfaces, saucier than ever.

I shake my head, freeing it from annoying *distractions,* "Sure. What would you like to know?" I say, taking a bite of cheese and crackers.

"Where were you born?"

"Okinawa, Japan. My parents, both in the US Air Force, met, married, and had me while stationed in Japan. We lived there until I was one."

"No kidding? That's fascinating! Ok, ready for the next question?" Jonathan asks, eating some of the pasta salad.

"Yep. Ready as I'll ever be."

"What made you decide to become a restaurant consultant?"

I nearly choke. I mean, how the hell am I supposed to reply without throwing myself under the bus?

Pretending to chew on some crackers, I cleverly buy myself a few seconds, as I shrewdly pull a believable response right out of my ass.

"Well, its funny. I never thought I'd be a restaurant consultant—I certainly didn't go to college specifically for that—but it's something I sort of fell into by chance. And...since then, I quite realize I enjoy helping someone take their business to the next level."

Jonathan nods, seeming to have bought the pile of crap I dished up on the fly.

"Ok, where did you go to college and what was your major?"

Shit. I can't *lie* about that, especially about my major. Being Kennedy Prescott is harder than I thought.

"I went to NYU with Sebastian and Gracie Winfield. My major was Journalism and my minor was Food Studies." I take a swig of wine, wishing it were something stronger, like tequila. Or poison. Anything to put me out of my misery.

Jonathan chuckles slightly. "Journalism and Food Studies? What an interesting combination. Olivia has her heart set on majoring in Journalism. How was NYU?"

"It's a great school. Hard at times, but I suppose that's not different from any other college," I answer, grateful he didn't probe deeper.

"So you and Sebastian, from Manifique, are pretty close?"

"Yep. We met at NYU and have been close ever since. I have no siblings, and any relatives I have are distant. He's filled in as friend, brother, and at times a parental figure, especially when it comes to advice."

Jonathan takes a sip of his wine and looks at me contently. "How did you find out your ex had cheated?"

I scoff, as I remember Garrett and that dumb chick. "I caught him in the act. And the event has been added to my 'why I hate Monday' list. At the time I was heartbroken. But now I see it as a blessing."

"How so?"

"The jerk fired me after I caught him with his assistant. And then Sebastian asked me to come on board as an independent contractor for the firm, and you are my first client. You, Jonathan Knight, are my blessing."

Jonathan smiles and kisses me. "Then I have to be sure to thank Sebastian for assigning you to me."

Time flies, as we chat more about me and my list of reasons why I hate Mondays, in which he finds amusing, The Hamptons, his troubles with Olivia, and Gracie Winfield.

"How do you know the Winfields?" Jonathan asks as we begin to pack up our picnic party.

"My parents and the Winfields, Randolph and Judy, served in the military together, for twenty years. They stayed in touch even when the Winfields fell into money and began investment banking that turned into the banking empire they operate today. Gracie went to NYU, but ran into trouble there, so Randolph threw her into banking. She operates the Winfield Bank and Trust branch near my house."

"Talk about a small world," Jonathan says with a pensive gleam in his eyes.

"It's a small world indeed."

We ride back to the building, making it just in time to meet the leasing agent.

"Mr. Knight?" the tall older woman says as we approach the building.

"Yes, thanks for meeting us here on such short notice. This is Kennedy Prescott," he says, and I shake her hand.

"Great to meet you both; I'm Valerie Mitchell, the leasing agent assigned to this property. It's been on the market for years. I almost forgot it was here, actually."

She takes us around the back, granting us entrance through the kitchen.

There are two grills, a four-vat deep fryer, a bunch of pans and utensils, dust everywhere and the usual prep sinks, hand sinks, dish sinks, walk-in cooler, walk-in freezer, a storage room, small office, and an employee restroom.

A wall and swinging door separates the back from the front where there is a long counter with a cash drawer, some tables, chairs stacked in a corner, more dust, cute mini-chandelier lights dropping from the ceiling, two small restrooms, and a mini bar. The space is definitely larger than I expected.

"What do you think?" Jonathan asks, grabbing my hand. He looks like a kid locked in a video game factory.

"No, what do you think?" I ask.

"Well, it needs some work, but I think the space is ideal for what I'm hoping to achieve."

He looks to Valerie, who is heavily engaged with something on her iPhone. "What are the lease terms, Valerie?"

"Oh yes." She lays her iPhone on the counter and retrieves a file folder from her purse. "Let's see here, the owner lists it as a month-to-month with an option to purchase. The month-to-month is $6000, which includes space rent from the land owner."

"Who is the land owner of this property?" I ask, curiously.

"We are–that is Winfield Bank and Trust."

"Of course," Jonathan remarks under his breath. He walks over to the window and peers outside, seeming to be in deep thought.

"Valerie, we'd like to see if we are a good fit, before committing to a traditional lease. Will the owner be interested in leasing the space to us through this weekend?" I ask, sensing Jonathan is too caught up on the fact the Winfields own the land this building sits on. "We'd clean up the place, and leave it in move-in ready form, should we prefer not to move forward." I add for good measure.

Jonathan turns to face me, smiles, and mouths the words *thank you*, to me.

Valerie takes a deep breath, in and out, as if my question has induced a mini panic attack. She picks up her iPhone, keying in a number. "Let me find out what I can do. This place has sat here, empty, for too long. Perhaps the owner is up for something–anything, that may help get this place leased, or better yet, sold. I'll be right back." She heads to the back, iPhone glued to her ear.

I walk over to Jonathan and rub his tense shoulders. "It will all work out, if it's meant to be," I say, unsure if I've helped put him at ease.

He pulls me into his arms, embracing me tightly. "I know, beautiful. I know."

Part Three

"*Eventually all the pieces fall into place... Until then, laugh at the confusion, live for the moment, and know that everything happens for a reason.*"

Carrie Bradshaw - Sex and the City

CHAPTER 23

*A*s a renowned food critic, never in my wildest of fantasies did I ever conclude I'd become a temporary partner in a new restaurant adventure.

Then again, never did I think I'd get fired, become a restaurant consultant to an irresistible chef I gave a poor restaurant review to, and fall head over heels for the irresistible chef—while pretending to be someone else.

Did I admit I'm head over heels?

Uh…yeah.

And who the hell knows how I'm going to get around Jonathan not knowing who I *really* am. I can't worry about that technicality just now. Although I did research the price to change my name to Kennedy Prescott. It may be a cost-worthy expenditure.

Now, my focus is how to support Jonathan as he toys with developing his Pop-up restaurant. The owner didn't want to venture into a concise short-term lease for one week. However, it was agreed to lease Jonathan (and his anonymous silent partner) the building for one month.

Oh and that anonymous silent partner? Yours truly. There was a snafu in the bank approval process that called for Jonathan needing a) someone to guarantee a loan b) a substantial down payment—which he could not pull together in the time needed to make this all happen —today.

So, I offered to assist and when I did, Jonathan was extremely reluctant. "I can't have you fund my venture."

And to that I opened up, explaining that for the last year, I have been afraid to spend one dime of the money I inherited when my parents died, and how his project has proven to be my purpose.

Reluctantly he agreed, vowing incessantly to pay me back in a couple of weeks. So, I excused myself while I called in a favor to Gracie Winfield, asking her to step into the working lease approval process, transferring money out of my hefty account, and writing me in as an anonymous and silent partner on the paperwork. Imagine the horror if my name—Penelope Monroe—could be seen by Jonathan on lease agreement paperwork?

Ugh.

How the heck did I get myself into this mess? And I don't mean the mess of being Kennedy Prescott. I could have easily never agreed to take on this assignment for Manifique. I mean how did I get myself in the mess of falling for someone who I know will never love the *real* me? And why have I fallen for him so soon?

"Kennedy, are you okay? You look pale." Jonathan asks, interrupting my internal pity party.

"Yes, I'm super fantastic," I reply.

Truth is I *am* fantastic, even though things have become slightly complicated.

Okay. Enough about all of that. It's been a few hours since Jonathan and I first looked at the building with Valerie, from going to the local real estate office with her to process paperwork, to finally getting approved for the one-month lease with an option to buy. We won't actually gain access into the building, with keys and all, until 9 a.m. tomorrow morning.

So now, the two of us are having a celebratory coffee across the street from Jonathan's new Pop-up restaurant. Well, *our* restaurant.

"Thank you again, Kennedy. And like I said, I'll pay you back in a couple of weeks." He reaches across the round wrought-iron table we are sitting at, taking a hold of my hand as we gawk like groupies at the restaurant across the way—ours, for the next month.

"Will we be able to set up everything in time for the grand opening this weekend?" I ask, my eyes still fixed on the empty building.

"I certainly hope so. I'll be able to gather a true assessment tomorrow morning, once we gain access."

"What are you going to name it?" I ask, thinking how thrilling it is to be a part of this terrific opportunity. I mean if all goes well, Jonathan can begin anew, making all of his goals and dreams come true.

"That's something I haven't thought yet. But it will come to me by tomorrow morning, I'm sure." He winks and smiles, taking a sip of his large cold brew. "You sure you're okay, beautiful?"

I nod, yes. "And all is okay with Knight and Daze, with your absence the rest of this week and this weekend?"

"Yep. I texted my chef and the manager. They have made sure all shifts are covered and that someone will be there every day to open and close."

"That's wonderful! I can't wait until we can get started."

"Me too. Yet in the meantime, I'm going to work on menu ideas and I'm hoping you can help me with a marketing plan?"

"Of course. Anything you need, I'm game."

He checks his watch, "We should probably get back to Brier Hill. Aunt Becca will be stoked that we'll be in town for the rest of this week, and I bet she'll be equally excited about the Pop-up restaurant idea. Plus, you'll be able to meet Uncle Joe and formally meet Olivia."

* * *

AUNT BECCA IS beside herself with joy, clearly evident as she jumps up and down after hugging and kissing both me and Jonathan on the cheek.

"What can I do to help? I've got extra supplies, a few vendors you can have access to, and of course we can all pitch in this weekend for the grand affair. Oooh, I even have spiffy, not-so-uniform-y uniforms you can wear."

"Thanks, Aunt Becca," Jonathan says, "we'll probably take you up on all those offers."

"Hello? We're home," says a man's voice, off in the distance.

"Honey, we're in the kitchen," answers Aunt Becca, her voice raised slightly. She looks to Jonathan and then to me. "That's Uncle Joe and Olivia. They're home!"

After Uncle Joe and Olivia say their hellos to Aunt Becca and Jonathan, I am introduced to them both. Uncle Joe gives me a hug—saying he's also a hugger, like Aunt Becca.

Olivia shakes my hand, looking at me with her head cocked to the side. "I think we've met before, no?" she asks, and I notice her pink hair and nose ring have disappeared.

"Uh yes," I say, "we met last week when I visited the restaurant. You served me, actually. But your hair looked a little different. The color in particular."

"Oh yeah. Aunt Becca said while I'm here I represent Brier Hill and she made me lose the nose ring and remove the pink streaks in my hair." She frowns, looking as though she lost a friend or something.

"Well, your hair looks absolutely lovely. And I hardly noticed your nose ring is no longer present."

She smiles softly and excuses herself, escaping up the stairs.

The four of us—Uncle Joe, Aunt Becca, Jonathan and myself move to the lounge where there is a piano, two cozy couches, a wood-burning fireplace, and a bar. We all get comfortable on the couches, as Jonathan begins to fill his uncle in on his plans for the restaurant.

"It was actually Kennedy's idea. She suggested I adopt this Pop-up concept to see if I have a chance at success here in town," he explains, placing his hand on my thigh.

"Sounds like a wise idea. What happens if you find your restaurant will be a success here?" inserts Aunt Becca.

Jonathan looks down, and I can tell a small piece of his joy has diminished. "If I'm successful, I'm prepared to sell Knight and Daze.

I've been receiving offers for quite some time now, but I've just been sweeping them under the rug."

"And your loft?" Uncle Joe asks, with his eyebrows raised.

"I'll sell that too, find a place in town or by the water, and let Olivia stay here while she finishes high school."

"Very well. Seems you've got it all figured out, which is wonderful. Just let us know what we can do to help. I'm so proud of you, Jonathan and your mom and dad would be too."

CHAPTER 24

"*I* totally owe you thirty-six bucks," I tell Sebastian after calling him via FaceTime a few seconds ago.

"Woman, it was beyond inevitable. I knew the chemistry between two hotties would result in the horizontal mambo. How was it? Did he give you a big O?"

I lower the volume on my phone and take my voice down to a whisper.

"Sebastian, I think I'm falling for him," I say, sinking into the covers on Jonathan's bed.

"So he *did* give you a big O. Honey, I'd fall for him too. Where is he now?" Sebastian asks, shoving a bite of pasta into his mouth.

"He's down at the shop, picking us out some clothes and other items we'll need while we are here for the rest of this week."

"Well, I love the plan about the Pop-up and I'm sure it will all go well. Want me to come up and help?"

"I'll let you know. But I will need help with some of the PR stuff, getting the word out about this weekend."

"Sure thing, love. Just send me a to-do list and I'll make it happen."

"Thanks, Sebastian. And I miss you."

"Me too, babe. And..." He pauses, taking another bite of pasta, "...

have you thought about a plan to keep your identity hidden, for the next hundred years or so?"

"No. And I can't worry about that now. Not until I get through this weekend, at least."

Sebastian shakes his head and rubs his temple, "Alrighty then, in the meantime, just go with the flow. If he makes you feel good, it will all work itself out. I promise. Anyway, I've gotta go now. HGTV's Property Brothers is about to invade my television. Ciao, babe."

Is it possible, I wonder, if this, whatever it may be, will all work itself out like Sebastian suggests? And if so, in whose favor? Surely, one of us is bound to get hurt, or perhaps both of us.

Hurt is inevitable, like crashing thunder after a lightning strike. Thunder has always frightened me and so has the thought of getting hurt.

I get comfortable, slipping into one of Jonathan's T-shirts before sinking back into his bed.

If all fails, at least I'll always have Brier Hill, the place where I let loose and fell—

Jonathan walks in with shopping bags, a bowl of strawberries, and a bottle of sparkling wine—a wonderful intrusion to my heady mindset.

"Sorry I took so long," he says, placing the shopping bags onto the bed. He holds up the bottle of wine and strawberries. "I thought we'd indulge a little…by the fireplace?"

"I love strawberries and wine," I tell him. "What's in the bags?"

"Oh right," he begins as he rummages through, pulling items out, one at a time. "Wine glasses of course, a pair of jeans like you requested, a couple of shirts, socks…you know, a few essentials."

I climb out of bed to put the goodies from the bags away, and Jonathan turns on the electric fireplace, sets up a blanket and some pillows, then disappears into the bathroom while I claim my spot by the fire. It seems crazy to want to sit by a fire in the summer, but the East Hampton coastal breeze lowers the temperature at night, and Aunt Becca keeps the air temp inside Brier Hill pretty crisp, so the soft, warm glow from the fire feels good.

Jonathan reappears, wearing only pajama bottoms, flaunting his ripped upper body as blatantly as a Las Vegas male stripper flashes his goods to an audience of horny women.

He pours us both some of the wine, hands me a glass, and positions himself next to me on the blanket, with the bowl of strawberries nestled between us. We both face the lustrous fire; its flames flicker and dance flirtatiously, a perfect representation of the two of us.

"It's been an eventful day," Jonathan says, as he feeds me a strawberry.

"Yep. It sure has. I didn't wake up this morning, expecting to be part owner of a Pop-up restaurant."

"Did you ever consider this is something you're meant to do? I mean be involved in the development and operations of a restaurant? You seem to know a lot about food; I sense your innate passion and appreciation for it."

I smile at his inference. Perhaps he's right. Maybe being a food critic was only prepping me for something deep within.

"Well, then if that's the case, I'll need to be less cooking impaired," I say, jokingly.

"I'll be more than elated to give you private cooking lessons, my sweet."

He swipes a long strand of hair off my face, tucking it behind my ear. And looks at me as though he's just realized something.

"Can I ask you a question?"

I can feel my heart begin to beat slightly out of rhythm. "Okay, what is it?"

"Do you really wear glasses?"

I chuckle a little. "Why do you ask?"

"Well, I could tell right off the bat, they didn't seem to fit you too well, which is why I made a comment about them. I was teasing you." He chuckles a little. "Then you showed up yesterday without them and you mentioned something about wearing contacts. Yet, since we've been here, I haven't seen you do anything contact-lenses related."

I pause briefly, taking a long sip of wine, "Okay, full disclosure.

And this is totally gonna sound crazy." I take a deep breath in and out. "Sebastian suggested I wear them, citing they made me look more businesslike. It's the PR person in him. He believes everyone should look their role. He even picked out my clothes. It's kind of who he is. And for the record, I hated those damn glasses." I smile, trying to assess his reaction. And just decide to take another long sip of wine instead.

Jonathan finally laughs and says, "I'm really glad Sebastian places so much care into his clients, which means I'm in good hands."

"Do you have more questions?" I ask, feeling a small buzz come over me. All of that wine I just inhaled.

"Yes. As a matter of fact I do," he says then pops a strawberry into his mouth. "Why are you attracted to me? And I know it's a pretty safe assumption, given, well, you know, how close we've become." He takes a swig from his glass of wine as if it were a self-reward for coughing up the nerve to ask me that poignant question.

I think for only a few seconds. "I'm attracted to you because somehow, you bring out someone in me I never knew existed. I feel as though with you I can escape some weird world I never belonged to and you're my new reality. I-I can't explain it other than that." I adjust the pillows and lie down, feeling the wine flow through me now more intensely. "And why are you attracted to me?" I manage through a melancholy whisper.

"Your tenacious ability to get to the bottom of things, for one," he says without hesitation. "I'm not one to open up, but y-you've managed to extract much more from me than anyone else."

He moves the bowl of strawberries that sits between us, and lays down next to me.

"You are the most ravishing woman I've met, and I want nothing more than to continue to learn even more about you. What makes you laugh, what makes you cry, and even what makes you angry," he says, his tone husky and low as the tips of his fingers slowly make their way from my leg, up to my outer thigh, until his hand reaches my hip.

I too want nothing more than to continue to learn all about him. Will I get the chance to? Or will everything change after this weekend, when we leave here and go back to the city? What if I just stop now? Open up and confess who I am?

And just as I'm about to open my mouth, almost conjuring up the nerve to tell him, he leans in closer, and we kiss, the light from the fire adding heat to the growing passion between us. He pulls me on top of him and as I sit straddled across the lower half of his body, I remove the T-shirt, exposing my breasts. He grabs them, gentle but forceful, lifting up his head, and I move in closer allowing his mouth to delicately devour my nipples. *You can't tell him now. Not ever,* my conscience reprimands.

I moan at his playful bites, and he turns me onto my back, slowly removing my panties. I anxiously help him ease out of his pants, freeing his manhood that I now so wholeheartedly crave. I lay straddled, patiently waiting for him to ease himself inside of me.

But instead, he's teasing, grinding against me as he moves his hands along the side of my breasts, and then back to my thighs.

"Please, I want you now," I beg hungrily.

But he doesn't give in.

"You have to be patient, baby. I want you too. But I so want this to last as long as it possibly can."

He moves down slowly, licking and kissing until he reaches my sweet spot and since he teased me up so fucking good, it takes only one lick and two sucks to bring me to a glorious high.

Then, he swoops in, taking me until he deservingly reaches his climax and softly whispers, "You see...patience is a freaking virtue."

* * *

"FOODIE CRUSH." Jonathan says, as we step out of the shower early the next morning.

"I'm sorry?" I ask, drying myself off.

"What if that's what we call the restaurant? Foodie Crush?"

"I like it. A lot," I admit, admiring the way his perfectly sculpted body looks when it's wet and naked.

"I'm glad you agree." His lips curve into a playful grin. "And don't look at me like that."

"Like what?" I giggle, hanging my towel on the hook by the open bathroom door.

"Like you want to throw me down and have your way with me."

"Well stop brandishing your sex gun around like *you* want me to throw you down and have my way with you."

He laughs. "My sex gun?"

"Yes," I say, backing out of the bathroom and into the bedroom as he walks toward me. "And don't you dare come any closer. Didn't you get enough of me in the shower?" I say, losing my footing, falling onto the bed.

"Ms. Prescott, I think I was pretty clear yesterday," he says, climbing on top of me, delicately kissing me on the lips. "I can never get enough of you."

CHAPTER 25

$\mathcal{T}$he next few days seem to charge by like a high-speed commuter train, as Jonathan and I work hard, preparing for the grand opening of Foodie Crush.

Between the two of us, things fall into place so quickly and so smoothly, it's hard not to believe this is only meant to be.

Once we gained access to the building, we quickly realized the owner left many usable pieces of equipment and supplies behind, which saved us money we set aside. We also came across a working wireless music system, elated that we'll be able to stream funky beats from an iPod, creating a buzzing atmosphere.

I discovered Olivia to be quite a sweet young lady, as the two of us got to know each other while we paired up to complete a thorough cleaning, set up tables and chairs, and make runs back and forth to local markets using the car Aunt Becca let me borrow.

Jonathan busied himself creating a slew of unique menu offerings. And as soon as the dishes were chosen, scrupulously developed, and tweaked to perfection, I forwarded the details to Sebastian. He then created a brilliant online campaign, complete with a dedicated website, a Facebook page, a Twitter account, and an Instagram page full of photos showcasing the dishes Jonathan skillfully prepared and artfully plated.

Sebastian also had storefront signage (a custom banner) and trendy menus sent to us via FedEx, and distributed a press release, which was, incidentally, picked up by *The East Hampton Sentinel* and the notable *New York Herald*, in which my idol, the acclaimed food critic, Gregory Hambrick, is employed.

Jonathan chose dishes he felt would best represent him as an innovative chef and a dedicated admirer of food; in my worthy opinion, his offerings are the Rolls Royce of comfort food:

APPETIZERS:
Stuffed Mac and Cheese
Pork Rinds
Duck Quesadilla
Entrees:
Backyard Burger (with pork and beef), served with truffle fries
Fried Chicken and Waffles
Fish Street Tacos (with radish)
Kobe Beef Street Tacos (with wicked salsa)
Turkey Cranberry Sliders
Desserts:
Tiramisu Cheesecake Bites
Mini Molten Caramel Cakes
As well as a full bar (That Uncle Joe will tend to) and a choice of soft drinks.

And now it's Saturday.

The day we introduce East Hamptoners' to Foodie Crush.

"Well, this is it, baby," Jonathan says, holding me close, as we stand in the middle of Foodie Crush, admiring all that's been accomplished in so little time. "Are you ready?" he asks, planting a kiss on my forehead.

"I am ready, and so happy for you. This is a dream restaurant. I know people are going to be giddy over your food."

Aunt Becca, Uncle Joe, and Olivia join us, and we have a group huddle as Jonathan reviews our roles for today and tomorrow.

"Okay, as a recap," he begins, "Aunt Becca and I will be in the kitchen, Uncle Joe, you've got drinks, and Olivia and Kennedy, you two lovelies will be hostesses and servers when we open at 11 a.m."

We make final touches, and when Olivia goes to unlock the doors, she lets out a muffled scream, "Oh my gosh, you guys, there is actually a long line. A *line*!!"

* * *

MOST WOULD SAY, to measure a restaurant's success, simply check the bottom line for profits. But to me, it's so much more than profitability—anyone can make a profit by cutting costs here and there, raising prices, reducing cost of goods, etc. Yet to me, a restaurant's true measure of success is by the look of pure eye-rolling gratification as the customer takes that first bite of their meal and when they walk out looking completely satisfied, as though they just got laid.

And that's exactly what I observed today. Everyone seems to be in love with Jonathan's food, the atmosphere, and the service.

It's been a nonstop force of energy since the time we opened the doors, and I couldn't be more enthralled as I've watched Jonathan in action inside of the kitchen and also as he's mingled unpretentiously with customers, speaking freely about his food and his plans for Foodie Crush.

At closing, the five of us are dead on our feet, and when we arrive back to Brier Hill, Jonathan and I make love, before we fall fast asleep.

Sunday is much of the same, except slightly elevated. More have turned out for the event, creating a longer-than-anticipated wait. But not one person seems to be agitated; most accepting the wait as part of the relishing experience.

Sebastian makes an appearance in the evening, and ends up tending bar with Uncle Joe, adding pizzazz to the night, before he drives back to the city.

We close at 8 p.m., and Jonathan sends everyone back to Brier Hill to rest, as the two of us stay behind and clean up.

"This has been a dream come true," he says, running his hands up and down my back, as we stand embracing in the Foodie Crush kitchen.

"I know, and I told you people would go crazy over your food. I'm so happy for you, Jonathan," I say, before he kisses me, unyielding passion flowing from his lips to mine.

Our lips reluctantly unlock, and Jonathan smiles as he looks down at me. "This would not have come together if not for you. Seriously, this was *your* idea, and Sebastian pulled through on the marketing side of things... I am utterly grateful."

"Do you know what you want to do? I mean, you think you'll sell Knight and Daze and make this a permanent gig?"

He smiles, with a pensive glow in his eyes. "Looks like that's a great possibility although I want to see how the next two weekends go. You're gonna help still, right?"

"Of course, I said I'm all yours for as long as you need me."

We discuss future goals and menu offerings as we continue to clean up when I develop a craving for coffee. The coffee shop across the street stays open late, and I offer to walk across and pick us both up a cup.

"I'll have a large, cold brew with a shot of vanilla," Jonathan shouts from the office as I head toward the front door.

"Okay, I'll be back in a flash," I say, feeling like nothing in the world could rip me off this puffy cloud nine I've been floating on for the past few days.

Jonathan makes me feel desired, loved, and needed as though I've been loved by him for my entire life.

I walk through the coffee shop doors, and a perky young woman greets me from behind the counter. "Hi! Welcome! Wow! You all were so busy. I stopped by before my shift today and I was blown away."

"Oh yes, we were extremely busy. How was your food?" I ask, even though the look on her face tells me she had an awesome experience.

"Oh my goodness. I had the Backyard Burger and Fries. It was too amazing. I mean, really. Food never tasted so good." She smiles genuinely.

"Great! I'll be sure to let the chef know," I say, a proud feeling running through my entire body.

"What can I get you tonight?"

"Oh yes. I'll have a large, cold brew with a shot of vanilla. And also a small mocha with cream," I tell her, lost in my own thoughts of yesterday and today.

"Awesome. And your name?"

"Penelope."

CHAPTER 26

*W*ith our two coffees in hand, I practically dance my way across the street and back into Foodie Crush.

Jonathan is waiting for me, wearing a euphoric grin, as he sits lounging comfortably at one of the tables.

I place the two drinks on the table and excuse myself briefly to visit the little girls' room.

As I make my way back around the corner from the restroom, I notice Jonathan's face has changed from its elated glow, to a look I have not seen, ever. It's like he's concerned and confused all at once.

Taking one small step at a time, I approach him ever so carefully. "Jonathan, i-is everything alright?" My voice cautious.

He stands up, both drinks on the table. He turns them around and points to the black ink on both cups.

I stare dismayed, stopping clear in my tracks.

Written on each cup in large black ink—the name PENELOPE.

Oh Fuck. *Fuck.*

While in the coffee shop, I was so distracted, cast-away in a sea of bliss, I didn't think twice when she asked me my name.

Jonathan looks at my guilt-stricken face as we stand staring at each other at least three feet apart, the farthest we've been since I've met him.

My eyes begin to fill with tears, as I feel my chest cave in.

No, please. Not now. You can't have a panic attack now.

Jonathan opens his mouth, and at first nothing comes out. Then finally, "W-what is this?" His voice timid and broken.

"I-I can explain," I begin. "You see—"

"No," he interrupts, his voice raised now, "you can't seriously be *her?*" He sits down and then stands right back up, now leaning against the table with his arms folded.

"Jonathan," I try again to explain, taking a step closer to him.

"No. Don't come near me right now, please. Just talk. Tell me what the fuck is going on here." His eyes fixed on me are dark and unforgiving.

"Jonathan, it's a long story, but I, agreed to be the one to help you since—"

"Since you ruined my life?" he practically yells. "What was all of this for? Out of pity? To clear your conscience? I opened up to you about *everything*. Shit, I fucking made love to you." He looks at me, frustration and hurt pouring through him. "Just when were you planning to tell me I was sleeping with the enemy?"

His words cut through me like a switchblade, fast and to the point.

And all I can do is run. Get the fuck out of here before I lose myself in this madness I created.

* * *

THE NEXT MORNING I wake up in my own bed, unable to open my eyes completely. They are swollen from all of the crying I did on the ride home via Uber, and all throughout the rest of the night as I tried unsuccessfully to fall asleep.

Thankfully, I was able to sneak in without waking Sebastian. A quick glance at the clock on my bedside table reveals it's now 11:30 a.m. The coast is definitely clear. Sebastian leaves for work at 8 a.m. sharp.

My heart aches. And so does my head…and my feet from running away from Foodie Crush, escaping the harsh reality I left behind.

I didn't mean for any of this to happen. All I wanted to do was help Jonathan turn his restaurant around. It's not like I planned for the two of us to fall into…whatever it was we fell into.

Lust?

Infatuation?

Love?

Ugh. Life sure has a way of knocking you down when you have nothing to hold on to.

My phone rings.

It's Sebastian.

"Hello?" I say, hoping he can't detect the despair in my voice.

"OMG, woman. Have you read the papers? As in *The Herald* and *The Sentinel?*" His voice sounds like he just discovered a winning lottery ticket.

"Nope. Not really. Why?"

"Well, shit! You all made the paper. Both of them! Foodie Crush is in news! A piece from some lowly food critic I've never heard of and another piece from none other than Gregory Hambrick. He gave it five freaking stars. One, two, three, four, *five*, Penelope. My boss is so freaking pleased, he's hinting at a promotion for me. So, I won't be home until much later. A staff celebratory dinner has been announced."

I sit up on the edge of my bed. "Are you serious? Well that's really great for you! And great for Jonathan. That's all such wonderful news."

"Yeah. He thought so too. I mentioned it to him this morning when he called me."

"Wait. Jonathan called you?"

Great, he probably spilled the beans and now Sebastian knows I've royally fucked up *everything*.

"Yep. He called asking for our address. Apparently you left in a hurry and forgot your bag and a few other things? Seriously. I had no idea you were home this morning. I would have totally made you an omelette."

I roll out of bed in a panic. "Wait. So he asked for our address to come *here*? Like *today*?"

"Uh, no. He said he was just going to send your stuff in a box via FedEx...something about being busy. Anyway, are you okay, Penelope? You sound so confused."

"I'm uh, I'm fine, Sebastian. But I've gotta go now. Love ya."

I end the call before Sebastian hears a yelp from my outburst of tears. Jonathan is sending me my things all packed up in a box. That's classic *it's over and I never want to see you again*, shit.

And perfect. Today's *Monday*.

I cry for a little longer before dragging myself into the bathroom and take a bubble bath, thinking this is the perfect time for Calgon to take me away. And I sit until the water turns cold, basking in pitiful somberness.

I force myself out, dry off, and grab my robe, putting it on as I dawdle into the kitchen for coffee.

What was I expecting? That Jonathan would show up with my stuff and confront me—tell me what a horrible person I am for stringing him along?

But it wasn't like that at all. I didn't string him along. I wanted so badly to tell him.

Through it all, this experience has taught me a great deal about myself. True, I've got a passion for food, but that doesn't mean I need to be this petty food critic, penning details of good, or bad meals. I've learned I can channel my passion for food from behind the scenes—right in the restaurant. I've also discovered I've developed an insane amount of feelings for Jonathan. So much that my mind, body, and soul are going through withdrawals right now.

Hmm.

And he said *I* was the one who was like a drug.

The Keurig completes its short brewing cycle and I grab my cup, adding two spoons of sugar and splash of cream.

A quick knock at the door startles me and I can't help but tremble. Could it be Jonathan? Did he come after all? Will he cut me as brutally as he did last night?

Only one way to find out.

Leaving my coffee behind, I run to the door and swing it open.

But it's not him.

It's the postman with a delivery for Sebastian.

Figures.

I sign for it and close the door and drag my ass all the way back to the kitchen.

After placing Sebastian's package on the counter and collecting my coffee cup, I move to the office. It's Monday. Time to post a review on my Facebook page.

An hour later, I press publish, sending my emotionally driven review out into the world, for all to see.

CHAPTER 27

The Fifty-Two Week Chronicles - Facebook Page
August 1, 2016

A spur of the moment adventure landed me in East Hampton, New York, last week where I was fortunate enough to spend time with what seems to have been a lifelong crush of mine—that is Foodie Crush.

It's a handsome little Pop-up in town for just a little while, to steal the hearts of locals and vacationers, making them drool over its fortuitous presence.

East Hampton seemed to be in shock as to how quickly this joint swooped in and made them all agog. They all hungered for something new, evident of how long they waited in line at their chance to get a taste.

Foodie Crush gave East Hampton exactly what they've been craving: satisfaction—expertly dishing out sultry menu offerings that are indeed the Rolls Royce of comfort food. From the decadent Backyard Burger to the sinfully rich Tiramisu Cheesecake Bites, you'll walk out heartbroken that you can't take your new crush with you.

I was lucky enough to get a backstage view of how the food was planned, prepared, and plated. The total experience was enough to sweep

*me off my feet and toss me into a whirlwind of culinary happiness. If I
had the chance to do it all again, I would.*

*Foodie Crush will be open every weekend for the rest of this month.
So, if you find yourself in East Hampton, stop by this little nugget of
five-star happiness. The talented executive chef, Jonathan Knight, would
love the opportunity to share his passion for food with you like he did
with me and the kind folks of East Hampton.*

Cheers to you and yours!

IT SEEMS as though hours have passed by as I loll on the living room
couch, trying to pry my eyes open. I cried until no more tears were
left, and I must have eventually fallen asleep. It's dark now and I don't
even know what time it is.

Do I even care?

Nope.

More sleep, off this hard couch and into my own bed, would be best.

But I'm too sore to move, still aching from this bloody heartache,
no doubt.

If Sebastian were here, he would have surely woken me up and
made me some sort of a heartbreak-curing smoothie, latte, or maybe
an omelette. But I remember he said he'd be home late, out for a staff
celebration dinner.

So it's just me. Wallowing all alone, and it's times like this when I
wish I had a cat or a dog (a hypoallergenic one, of course). Shit, even a
fucking goldfish would do.

Ugh. Enough.

I push myself off of the couch and then…lie right back down.

I have no energy.

A classic case of Jonathan Knight Withdrawal Syndrome.

I acquiesce, give into my sorrow, and pull a throw over my
entire body.

I'll just wait for Sebastian to come home.

He'll know what to do.

I doze off momentarily, then hear a faint knock at the door.

Sebastian. He's probably drunk from his celebration dinner and can't find his keys.

I get up, turn on the hall light and hurry to the door.

Before I reach it, there's another knock. "Hold on, Sebastian, I'm coming," I mutter.

I swing open the door and—

"Hi," Jonathan says, his voice much more delicate now than it was last night. He holds up my bag and says, "You left this behind."

I stare at him, utterly shocked, but try hard to pretend I'm unfazed by him being here. At my door. Looking all...Jonathan like.

"Uh, yeah. I suppose I did," I say, unclear of what my next move should be. Do I snatch the bag from his hands and slam the door in his face? Or do I run into his arms and beg him to forgive me?

"Um, can I come in?" he asks.

"Oh, of course," I say, widening the door's opening. I step aside, allowing him entrance.

We stand in the hall for a minute as I adjust my robe, and seconds later, I finally take my bag from his hand. Feeling uneasy from the awkward silence that lingers, I walk down the hall, toward the kitchen, not knowing exactly what to say, and hear Jonathan's footsteps following close behind me.

"Can I get you something, some water, a cup of coffee, soda?" I offer as I motion for him to take a seat on one of the barstools.

"N-No thank you. I-I, uh, only came to give you your bag," he says as he sits and begins to nervously tap his fingertips on the countertop.

"Oh. Well, thank you. That was quite thoughtful."

I take a seat in the barstool next to him, facing him, our knees now touching. He looks at me and I notice his eyes are slightly red. Either he shed a few tears of his own, or he got high. I laugh internally, knowing Jonathan certainly did not get high.

"Sebastian said you were going to send me my stuff," I say, glancing at the clock on the microwave that says 8:03 p.m.

"I thought about that, but decided I would rather hand your stuff over to you in person."

I nod and put my bag down, realizing I had been gripping it close to my chest.

My nerves taking over.

"I read the review you posted today. For Foodie Crush. Thank you for that," he says, still nervously tapping his fingertips on the counter.

"You're welcome. That post will probably be the last time I post for a while. I'll send something out tomorrow to my followers," I admit, now joining in with the finger tapping.

"Why? I mean why the last post?"

"It's just not who I am anymore. You made me realize that."

He raises his eyebrows briefly. "And who are you?"

"That's what I need to find out," I say, shrugging my shoulders.

A lengthy pause almost steals the moment, like a vulture swooping down on its prey.

"I'll tell you who I think you are." He stops tapping his fingers along the counter, and rests his hands onto his lap. "You are this incredibly talented woman who seems to handle whatever is thrown at her. I thought about this during my two-hour ride here. I mean, you were a food critic who, even though you probably knew it was risky, agreed to help the same chef you thought you'd destroyed. You *had* to go in undercover, so to speak, in order to make it work. I can't blame you for that. And I can't blame you for what happened between us, because we both allowed it to happen. It's what we wanted and quite frankly needed. And then, you still found it in you to post a review about the total experience, even after you got hurt."

I look at Jonathan and all I can do is cry. And I thought I was all out of tears.

"I'm so sorry I yelled at you," he says, grabbing a hold of my hand.

I wipe my face with the sleeve of my robe.

"It's okay. And I'm sorry about everything, Jonathan."

"Everything?" he asks, raising up from the stool, easing closer to me. He works his way between my legs, grabbing a hold of my chin, to gently lift my head.

"Please don't be sorry about everything. I know I'm not. In fact, I lied. I didn't come here only to give you your bag. I came here because, well, first of all, I know how much you hate Mondays. I didn't want to be added to your reasons why list." He chuckles at his comment. "I also came here because—"

He stops and takes in a deep breath. "Penelope," he continues, and the sound of him saying my *real* name puts me in a spiral, "I'm so fucking in love with you."

His lips curve into that sexy smirk that makes me all google-eyed.

"You're in love with me?" I repeat, holding my hand to my chest, as it beats out of control.

"Yes, with you, Penelope Monroe. Everything about you. The way your eyes smile when you see me, the fact that we share losing our parents in common, the way your face lights up when you taste something delicious, the way you moan when I make love to you, and the way you intoxicate me, making me feel like I can never get my fill of you."

He pulls me in closer to him, leans over, and kisses me hard and sensual.

And when we finally break free, I catch my breath and tell him exactly how I feel.

"I-I'm in love with you too."

After he playfully asks me where he can *take* me, Jonathan whisks me off to my room and the two of us lose ourselves in each other for hours on end. And through our lovemaking, Jonathan proves over and over again how powerfully love can conquer hate.

And now, today, meet the new me: Penelope Monroe, the unbroken-hearted food critic, turned love-crazed restaurant consultant, turned part restaurant owner.

And, oh yeah…

I fucking *love* Mondays.

EPILOGUE

Three Months Later...
Garrett Harrison

It's true, you know...not realizing what you have until it's gone, as cliche as it may fucking sound.

I came across a wedding announcement today, as I picked up the newspaper, hoping to successfully peruse the job section—for any job, since I'm now gainfully *unemployed*.

Jake fired me from *The Hudson News Bee* a few months ago. Can you believe that shit? I thought I was like a son to him. He claimed the fact I couldn't seem to keep my dick in my pants was bad for the newspaper. I told him he should start hiring less attractive women... and that seemed to piss him off even more. So much so, he sent me off without a severance package or a letter of reference.

Whatever.

Anyway, back to this wedding announcement thing. I admit, even though I'd like to consider myself to be an emotionally strong man, seeing it has woosied me up. Big time.

You see, I used to date this beautiful and talented journalist named Penelope Monroe who Jake and I hired to write a weekly restaurant review column. She quickly became this renowned food critic, surpassing our expectations.

Jake and I both discovered Penelope's talents were too grandiose for such a measly periodical, like *The Bee*. Yet, her column alone perked up sales and ratings, so there was no fucking way we were going to let her go.

And dating her was purely accidental. I mean, it's true, I wanted to hook up with her the moment I laid eyes on her when she walked into *The Bee* for a job interview. She was hot. Not an average kind of hot. Explosive.

But I was careful to keep my distance; in other words, I made every effort to keep our relationship strictly business. However, one evening, the two of us were working late and we decided to go out for a bite to eat.

Now mind you, it had been almost six months into our working relationship, and I knew nothing about Penelope, not even how she took her coffee (which, by the way, is two sugars and cream).

Dinner lasted for hours, as I got to know her...and just how amazingly captivating she was. So, I asked her out again and a couple of dates later, we became an item. I knew I was this player, who for ages toyed with women without any regard to their feelings. But she was the one. The one who would tame the lion.

Or so I thought.

I allowed the pesky green monster—jealousy—to intervene.

It all began when Gregory Hambrick, a popular food critic who worked for *The New York Herald*, called me. Somewhere, in our conversation, Gregory mentioned he was close to retirement and would very much like to see *The Bee's*, very own Penelope Monroe step in and take his place. He said *The Herald* was even willing to buy out her remaining contract. He had read all of her reviews and was quite taken with her writing.

I was like, really?

And...then I quickly told him hell-fucking-no.

Of course, I never bothered to mention that phone conversation to

Penelope, or to Jake for that matter. I selfishly didn't want to risk her jumping ship.

However, that particular phone call was a huge eye-opener for me. I realized then, Penelope was just too damn good for me.

Naturally, I reverted back to my playboy habits and began screwing a ton of women, behind Penelope's back. I became relatively distant even though, deep down, I knew if she caught me, she'd get hurt.

Things got hot and heavy one evening between me and my newly hired editorial assistant. I admit, I didn't hire that chick for her work-related skills. I hired her because I thought she had nice boobs. Somehow that evening's 'sexcapade' adventure landed us straight in Penelope's office. I figured it was okay, because Penelope had already left for the day. And I was too far into the moment to change course.

But as fate would have it, Penelope forgot her journal. She returned to her office just as I pinned my assistant's cute naked ass onto the desk, me in between her thighs, her legs and those sexy five-inch stilettos high in the air, my shirt off, and my pants right at my ankles.

I'll never forget the look on Penelope's face.

A look of disgust, pain, and hatred all bundled up.

I thought the right thing to do was fire her. Penelope, that is.

I mean, I totally figured she'd land on her feet, since she was this sought-after food critic. I never heard from her or saw her since that day, assuming all this time she went on to work for *The Herald*.

Until today. As I come across this surprising wedding announcement that just so happens to have made the front page of *The Herald*.

And what does it say?

Headline: *Five-Star Celebrity Chef Jonathan Knight Ties The Knot With Gorgeous Renowned Food Critic Penelope Monroe—Rivals No More*

Celebrity Chef Jonathan Knight married who he referred to as the woman of his dreams, during a small ceremony in front of their East Hampton waterfront home, last weekend.

The two met under serendipitous circumstances after she left a small newspaper where she wrote a popular restaurant review column to begin working for PR Firm Manifique as a Restaurant Consultant.

Jonathan Knight was her first assignment and, as luck would have it, Jonathan was the chef and owner of Knight and Daze Grill and Bar—a restaurant Penelope Monroe publicly abolished via her well-known weekly column that boasted over 900k followers.

The two quickly connected and fell head over heels in love, putting their rivalry on the chopping block.

Jonathan and Penelope now own and operate the successfully posh new restaurant—Foodie Crush in East Hampton, New York.

Jonathan says he owes their meeting to PR mastermind, Sebastian Taylor Ramos, who now heads up Manifique's west coast branch in San Francisco, California.

Knight and Daze Grill and Bar was sold, and is now owned and operated by a well-known celebrity who also purchased Jonathan's pricey TriBeCa loft as part of the hefty real estate transaction.

Penelope Monroe has recently become involved in several philanthropical ventures, putting money she inherited to use and her popular Facebook Food Blog Page—The Fifty-Two Week Chronicles—is being run by her sister-in-law, Olivia Knight, who hopes to follow in Penelope's footsteps as a journalistically inspired food critic.

Jonathan and Penelope say they plan to expand Foodie Crush next year and are currently mentoring new chefs, gearing up for that expansion.

The lovebirds also say when visiting East Hampton, feel free to stop by Foodie Crush. They are having a Wedding Bells menu special all month long.

Seeing Penelope in the newspaper all aglow makes me happy and sad at the same time. Which is why I'm all woosied up. I should have held onto her.

But life is what we make it and I've made mine what it is today. Maybe I should keep my dick in my pants and wait for Ms. Right to mosey on into my life? Or maybe I should continue to be myself because life is too damn short.

Besides, I am having a blast going out on Tinder dates. The women I'm meeting are sweet, sexy, and exciting.

Penelope had a favorite quote she once shared with me—"Some people refuse to settle for anything less than butterflies."

Looks as though Penelope Monroe has found her butterflies...

* * *

Greetings,

I truly hope you have enjoyed reading THE FIFTY-TWO WEEK CHRONICLES!!

I had an absolute ball writing about Penelope and Jonathan's whirlwind romance - I hope you fell in love with their story.

I am working on the next book in the Delectables in the City series...

A Cupcake and a Gentleman, in which I hope to release this Fall. YAY!

In the meantime, releasing September 17, 2017 is CINDERELLA-ISH which you can pre-order now on Amazon for only 99 cents — Cinderella-ish

If you're interested in receiving updates on the progress of the next book, please sign up for my Members Only Group - you can find the signup page on my website: https://www.joslynwestbrook.com/signup

Thank you so much for reading my debut novel! I look forward to creating more stories with captivating and witty characters for you to enjoy!

xo **Joslyn**

Published by Fifth Avenue Publications.

Cover design by pro_ebookcovers

Edited by Indie Editing Chick

First Edition (Jan 2017) Complete First Edition (May 2017)

www.joslynwestbrook.com

❋ Created with Vellum

ABOUT THE AUTHOR

Joslyn Westbrook has been creating stories since grade school. Her passion for writing often led to teachers and college professors reading her stories to the class, showcasing her creativity. Putting her writing on hold, Joslyn pursued a career as a Business Consultant as she raised her children. While she enjoyed working with business owners, she craved what she believed was her true calling - writing. During her free time, Joslyn began writing her romance and series of sexy chick-lit style novels to curb her passion for writing. Her work as a Business Consultant has spawned the concept of several characters featured in her books. Joslyn is a self-proclaimed foodie, enjoys shopping, cooking, binge watching on Netflix, and spending time with her husband and children at home in sunny California. This is Joslyn's debut novel.

You can connect with Joslyn via the links below:
www.joslynwestbrook.com
joslyn@joslynwestbrook.com

Made in the USA
San Bernardino, CA
17 August 2017